Angelhood
A.J. Cattapan

Vinspire Publishing

www.vinspirepublishing.com

ISBN: 978-0-9903042-6-5
PUBLISHED BY VINSPIRE PUBLISHING, LLC

May you realize you are never alone,
even on your darkest days.

A.J. Cattapan

Chapter One

Getting the gun is easy. Mom has never tried to hide it from me and my sister. As soon as Dad moved out three years ago, she bought it for our "protection."

In her bedroom, I slide open the top dresser drawer and pull out a skeleton key attached to an angel key ring. The angel is made of pewter and smiles at me knowingly. I hate its smile. At the foot of Mom's bed, I kneel in front of Grandma's old cedar chest. I run my fingers over the rose design that disguises the keyhole. After slipping in the skeleton key, I turn it and listen for the click. It's easy to hear in our quiet suburban home.

The heavy lid creaks as I open it. A faint cedar scent escapes. When I was little, Mom told me cedar chests were supposed to hold a woman's most treasured items before and after she married — lace tablecloths, fine linens, dresses, photos. We don't have much of that. Instead, Mom has filled Grandma's cedar chest with our old report cards and baby books, a lock of chestnut hair from my first haircut, the First Communion dress both Cecille and I wore, and our baptismal candles. I dig deeper. Somewhere in this chest is a shoebox. And in that shoebox is a .38 snub-nosed revolver wrapped in a kitchen towel.

The cedar chest actually contains several shoeboxes. Taking the lid off the first one, I find programs from all the plays I've been in. On top is the program for *Arsenic and Old Lace*, the play I was in last weekend. Actually, I'm supposed to be in it again tonight, but that's not going to happen. I put the cover back on the box and push it aside. Leaning around the lid of the cedar chest, I check the time on Mom's alarm clock. Three minutes after five. It's Friday afternoon. Mom's already turned off her computer at her desk outside Mr. Henderson's office. She's probably already headed toward the parking lot. That gives me 22 minutes — give or take a few, depending on traffic lights — before she gets home.

I reach for the next shoebox. It contains two tiny pairs of shoes. Cecille's first pair of ballet slippers were pale pink with white bottoms that went gray from hours of pirouetting and pliéing. They were well loved and well worn. My first tap shoes, on the other hand, are still shiny and barely scuffed. They were unloved and worn poorly. I put both pairs of shoes back in the box, but linger on the ballet slippers for a moment. When I'm gone, Mom will be able to afford the best ballet school for Cecille, the one that practically guarantees she'll get into Julliard. My sister will be a success. Someone in the family should be.

Before I can pull out the third shoebox, a drawing peeking out from under the report cards distracts me. I recognize it instantly. A homework assignment from my sixth grade Religious Ed class. I smile as I remember how angry I'd been…

"Homework?" I had whined to my best friend Ally. "We shouldn't get homework in Religious Ed."

Luckily, Ally had a way of looking on the bright side. She invited me to her house for a sleepover so we could work on the assignment together. After homemade pizzas and ice cream sundaes, Ally and I pulled on our cuddly pj's, and spread Ally's markers and colored pencils all over her family room floor. The assignment was to draw what we thought heaven would be like.

Lying on our bellies, we pulled blank pieces of white paper in front of ourselves and began sketching. Multi-level cloud platforms came first. Some were high, some were low, some were connected by cloud escalators, but they wouldn't really be used since we'd all have wings then.

Next, we worked on what each cloud would contain. I

insisted that one cloud would simply be stocked with *3 Musketeers* candy bars, their fluffy insides like little clouds of chocolate heaven all on their own. Ally wanted a cloud that came up with a different kind of candy every day of eternity so she'd never get bored. We both wanted clouds where bands could serve up dance music so the party could last forever. Of course, we'd all be wearing the latest fashions, and we'd all look like ourselves, only better—no acne and no frizzy hair. "And no glasses!" Ally insisted as she pushed hers higher on her nose.

After a while, we got so into the project that I forgot all about being mad at Mrs. Dolan for assigning homework. When I'd finished filling in the 24/7 fast food cloud, I peeked at Ally's drawing. On a cloud in the center, Ally had drawn her mom, her dad, her older brother Joey, and their cat Gloria. I looked back at my drawing. Mine had no family, but that didn't surprise me. Mom and Dad fought all the time. And Cece was such a baby—only six at the time—that all she ever did was follow me around and annoy me to death.

"Do you think when we get to heaven, it'd be all right if I stay with your family all the time?"

Ally looked up from her drawing, her eyes wide. "Don't you think your family's going there?"

I shrugged. "Who knows? But even if they do, I'd still rather be with yours."

"Oh." Ally scratched the back of her head by sticking the capped end of a light blue marker through her jet-black hair. "I'm sure you could stay with us. It's heaven. Doesn't that mean you get whatever you want?" Ally went back to coloring in the background.

"Do you ever wish you could go to heaven right away?"

Ally scrunched up her nose. "You mean, die?"

I snorted. "No, I don't mean the dying part. I mean the everything-being-perfect part. No more school. No more annoying little kid sister. No more bossy parents or teachers."

"I don't know." Ally bit her lip. "Earth has good stuff too. And we're not here very long to enjoy it. We'll have all eternity to enjoy heaven."

Ally had a point.

"Do you believe all that stuff about when you die there's a white tunnel of light and then you see all the people you knew who died before you?" I had finished my drawing, so I sat up and signed my name on the back.

Ally still lay on her stomach. "I don't know. Maybe."

"I hope so. It'd be pretty scary if all you saw was a bright light, but you didn't see anyone you knew. I wonder who'd greet me. My parents would probably be off fighting on a cloud somewhere and forget to show up."

Ally sat up, too. "I'll tell ya what. If I die first, I'll be sure to be there when you enter the light." It was the perfect thing to say, but then again Ally had been the perfect best friend.

Sitting beside Grandma's cedar chest, I can't stop the tears from coming. One of the tears drops onto the heaven drawing on my lap. Too many things have changed in the past six years. Another glance at the clock tells me the time is 5:15. I'd better hurry. Mom'll be home in another ten minutes. I lay the heaven drawing on top of the report cards and reach for the third and final shoebox. The gun has to be in here. My hands tremble a little as I take it out. When Mom bought it, she'd said we were never to touch it because guns weren't for little girls, but I'm seventeen and hardly little anymore.

Sitting on the edge of Mom's bed, I lift off the box's lid and then pull out the gun wrapped in a green-striped kitchen towel. It's heavier than I expected. I unwrap the towel and let the revolver fall into my right hand. I consider putting everything away, but what's the point? They'll know soon enough what I did.

Remembering the instructions I'd read online, I push the

latch on the left side of the gun and swing open the cylinder. The gun has two rounds in it. One more than I'll need. I snap the cylinder closed and head out of the room. At the doorway, I stop, turn around, and pick up the heaven drawing before heading out again. I'll know soon enough how close I came to being right.

In my room, I lay everything out on my bed—the note I've written to explain everything to Mom, the Chicago Tribune article about the car accident, the obituary from the Pioneer Press, the .38 snub-nosed revolver, and the drawing of heaven. I have a faint memory of Mrs. Dolan saying suicide is a sin, but that's only if your reasons are selfish. Life will be better for my sister when I'm gone. Mom will finally have the money to send her to proper ballet classes. At least one of us can become a successful artist. Mom deserves that. She deserves at least one child who isn't a failure. Not to mention a killer. The tips of my fingers graze the obituary, and I choke back tears. Yes, the world will be a safer place when I'm no longer here.

My heart pounds in my chest. Funny how the body fights to live even when the mind knows it must die. I raise the gun and am surprised how far I must stretch my index finger to reach around the trigger. I lift the gun to my head just as I hear keys scrape into the front door downstairs. Mom's home early. It's now or never.

"God, forgive me," I whisper and squeeze the trigger.

They say your hearing is the last to go when you die. And they're right. After the bang from the gun subsides, I hear footsteps running up the stairs. The last thing I hear is a high-pitched scream.

Oh God, what have I done?

Chapter Two

Something went wrong. This isn't right. I should be floating away on a cloud into a sea of light. Instead, utter blackness fills my vision. The void is so complete I can barely tell whether or not I exist. Or if I ever existed at all. What on earth have I done?

Suddenly, there are flashes of life. Episodes from a life that are not my own. They come at me so suddenly it's as if someone hit play in a darkened movie theater, and the film picked up in the middle of a scene.

I see a girl. She's several years younger than me. Maybe fourteen. Mousy brown hair, pulled back in a small ponytail.

She's in a house. It's dark outside the kitchen window where she's making mac-n-cheese for dinner. A man walks in. He's tall with a graying beard and mustache. He sets down a yellow construction hat on the table. The man must be her father, but there's no greeting from either of them. He grabs two plates from a cabinet and places them on the table. Cups, silverware, and a gallon of milk follow. The girl spoons the mac-n-cheese onto the plates. Not a word is spoken between them.

The scene disappears and everything fades to black. As I wait for the light to reappear, I question my existence. Is this a dream? I killed myself.

Didn't I?

The movie jolts to life. The girl sits in a classroom, copying math problems from the board. I move closer to her, but it's not my body moving. More like I'm working a movie camera, gliding down a dolly track to focus on my target. As I watch over her shoulder, she pulls out a black notebook. The cover design appears to be a hot pink heart, but the swirly lines that make up the heart look more like thorny vines. In the margin of her notebook, she scribbles book titles: *Jane Eyre, Pride and Prejudice, A Walk to Remember, Thirteen Reasons Why.*

Blackness. This time I'm left in the dark so long, I almost forget about the girl.

The next vision shows me a crossword puzzle, and for a moment I think I'm finally seeing something other than the nameless girl's life. But then the camera zooms out, and I see her tapping her pencil against her ponytail. She sits on a twin bed covered with a pink comforter. Piles of well-worn paperbacks are stacked where a nightstand should be. A cheap black alarm clock rests precariously on top. The girl flings the puzzle aside and pulls up a canvas bag from the floor. She reaches inside and pulls out a stapled set of papers. My view shifts so that I swing around her. At the top of the page in pretty blue ink the words "Please see me" are written in neat cursive letters. The girl crumbles the pages, throws them and the bag onto the floor, and crawls under the covers.

The darkness returns, but only for a short while.

She's in the kitchen again. In fluffy pink slippers and sheep-adorned pajamas, she pads her way across the room. She pulls a knife from the magnetic strip that hangs over the sink. She heads out, knife in hand, flipping the switch as she goes. The way through the hall is dark, but I can hear the rubber bottom of those pink slippers on the wooden floor. A light is flipped, and she stands before a mirror in a tiny white and blue bathroom.

As she stares at her reflection, I realize my image is not reflected in the mirror. Even though I'm right behind her, all I see in the mirror are her red-rimmed eyes, her stringy brown hair, and those blasted sheep pajamas.

What happened to *my* eyes, *my* hair, and *my* body? I know I'm dead, but shouldn't I see something in the mirror? I used to have the shiniest chestnut hair, and I'd braid a few small strands at the front to create depth in my otherwise flat mane. And my eyes were big and brown with thick lashes. Looking at the pathetic girl in front of me, I realize I never appreciated how pretty I actually was. No model, that's for certain. But no train wreck either.

In front of me, the girl looks down at her left wrist and then pulls the knife closer to her eyes to examine its blade. Like a surgeon inspecting her instruments before operating, she runs a finger along the knife's edge. Then she holds the flat edge of the blade against her left wrist, and I scream, begging her to stop, but it's the proverbial nightmare problem. I feel the shriek deep in my soul, but no sound follows.

Blackness curls around the edges of my vision when another voice cries out.

"Vera!"

The girl looks up. The knife is thrown into a small drawer under the sink just as the tall man with the graying beard walks in.

"Vera, what are you doing up?"

The girl doesn't answer. She simply flips the light switch and walks out.

Blackness again. At least now I know her name.

Something about the last scene brings back memories. My vision has changed. What I see now is my own life. Not Vera's. The most recent memories come first.

On my bed is the note I scrawled on a page torn from my English notebook. It lists all the reasons I hated my life. Next to it rests the heaven drawing and the newspaper clippings from the car accident. Once again, I can feel the cold metal of the trigger, and I remember how far I had to stretch my petite fingers to make the gun go off. For the briefest moment, I can smell the smoke and hear the high-pitched scream that followed, and then the darkness surrounds me once more.

The other details of my life are fuzzy. I know I was unhappy. That is more than obvious, but at the moment all I really remember is anger. Anger directed toward God. He had failed me, I was sure.

And now where is He? Where am I for that matter? If I'm dead, shouldn't I be somewhere other than Earth? Watching periodic episodes from a girl's life interspersed with inky darkness and memories from my own life certainly isn't what either Ally or I had imagined heaven would be, and yet I'm certain this can't be hell either.

I move my hands to see if I can feel my way through the night that surrounds me, but there's nothing there. Panic sets in. What if I'm stuck in the darkness for good? Is that even possible? I was taught in Religious Ed classes that God is light. Does this endless darkness mean there is no God?

Before I can even finish the thought, the girl's bedroom reappears. She has pulled the pink comforter up around her neck, and in the moonlight that peers through her bedroom window, I can see a tear rolling down her cheek.

"Oh, God," Vera gasps. Her voice is low, but I can hear her plainly. "Why am I so alone?"

I glide to her bedside. She is petite, like my little sister. I want to sit on the edge of her bed, hold her hand and tell her that she's not alone, that I'm here. I reach for her only to remember that I have no hands, no body, no voice. Instead, I stay by her bed, listening to her gasping sobs, watching her toss and turn, until finally exhaustion consumes her and she falls asleep.

Chapter Three

Before I know it, I'm hovering in a classroom again. This time it's not math. Dickinson, Shakespeare, and Frost smirk at me from the walls. The desks and room design look vaguely familiar, and I realize I'm in my old high school.

Although I recognize the building, I do not remember this particular teacher. She is younger than my mom, but clearly not a brand new teacher. As she talks to the class, she tucks her bobbed auburn hair behind her ear. She is round-faced and could probably stand to lose a few pounds, but something makes her instantly relate-able.

"I'd like us to read this poem aloud, stanza by stanza, to really delve into its meaning." She holds the fat teacher's edition of the text in both hands and looks over her students. "Vera, will you take the first stanza, please?"

My focus shifts to the girl with the mousy brown ponytail in the third row. Startled, she looks up from her book, her eyes wide with fear. The teacher waits. Several members of the class turn to look at Vera. Her eyes flicker from one classmate to another, and then she looks back at her teacher, whose eyes have not left Vera.

Finally, Vera looks down at her book and begins to read. "Because I could not stop for Death,/He kindly stopped for me/The Carriage held but just Ourselves." Vera pauses, her mouth hanging open for a moment. "And…*Immortality*."

The girl in the cheerleader uniform in front of Vera turns around and raises her eyebrow. Did she find Vera's emphasis of the last word as eerie as I did?

Immortality? Is that what I am experiencing? For millennia, humans have dreamed of being immortal, but is this what it means? Floating back and forth between random acts on Earth and a sheer and utter blackness that lasts so long, panic rises in a throat that no longer exists? If immortality means watching periodic episodes from a life you don't know, I don't think the ancient Egyptians would have revered it so much.

The teacher pulls her eyes away from Vera to look at the rest of her class. "How does Emily Dickinson portray death in this first stanza?"

Vera raises a tentative hand, but the teacher calls on a tall boy from the opposite side of the room.

"She's personifying death. She's making it sound like a person who is coming to take her away on a trip."

"Yes, Josh. This is an example of personification. What else is Dickinson trying to say?"

Vera's is the only hand up now. "Vera?"

"Dickinson says the carriage holds death, herself, and immortality. Doesn't that mean death is actually making her immortal? He's bringing her to a place where she can live forever without the pain of life as we know it."

I remember the scene from the bathroom with the knife. Surely, that's what Vera had been hoping for. Eternity without the pain of life. That's what I'd been hoping for when I pulled the trigger. But it wasn't what I got. Instead, I got this—and I'm not even sure what this is yet.

Like Vera, I look to the teacher for answers, but she seems to be having problems finding an answer too. Her mouth opens, then closes.

A rushing wind roars through the corridor outside the classroom. It reminds me of that tornado movie last year. My first thought is that the roof has blown right off the building, but then I look around and see that no one else is startled by the sudden noise. Can't they hear it too?

I glide toward the door to see what is happening, but before I reach it, billowing black smoke pours into the room, pushing me back. The smoke is shapeless at first, but it starts to twist upon itself, almost like a funnel cloud. The dark shadow hovers just inside the doorway like black smoke lingering over a fire, only there's no flame below.

To my surprise, the shadowy cloud goes unnoticed by the living beings in the room.

"I don't think that's what Dickinson was saying," continues the teacher.

"But look at the rest of the poem," says Vera. "She's not frightened of death. She seems to welcome it. She wants the immortality that follows death."

While Vera is talking behind me, I stare at the black cloud. It hovers within a couple feet of the doorway before moving down the aisle. Its shape changes again. No longer a funnel cloud, the smoke becomes a cloaked figure. Under the hood, a face forms. The ghostly image is that of a girl about my age, but her skin is so taut that she's almost skeletal. Her thin lips are drawn tightly, and her eyes are hollow. Instinctively, I plant myself between the shadowy specter and Vera. I don't know who she is or what she wants, but I can't imagine this shadow of a soul bringing anything good.

"I think you're right, Vera. The speaker of the poem isn't frightened. Perhaps she is comforted by the idea of death." The teacher's tone has changed. She sounds almost wistful. "Perhaps she did suffer in life, and now she is free from her suffering."

Suddenly, the smoky shadow shifts directions and moves toward the teacher. My first thought is that of relief. Maybe the shadow girl isn't interested in Vera after all, but then I begin to wonder what she wants with the teacher. What will happen when the shadow reaches her, and why doesn't anyone notice the evil lurking in the room? Her presence is so menacing I wonder how the living beings in the room can't sense it at all.

The smoky shape slides closer to the teacher, and I

consider leaving Vera to block the specter's way when a bright light shimmers in the gap between the teacher and the shadow girl. The light seems to hold no shape; it simply emanates from a spot midair. The shadow girl slows down. The light shimmers again, and two flashes of light spread out like wings unfurling from the glow's center, stopping the shadow girl in her tracks.

"Then again," continues the teacher, "I'm not sure Emily Dickinson was trying to say she really *wanted* death."

"But look at how she ends the stanza," cries Vera, and the specter swirls before turning toward her. "She writes 'And Immortality' all by itself on a separate line. Poets only separate words like that when they want to make them stand out. Immortality is important to her. She wants it. She wants Death."

The shadow girl heads Vera's way again. She opens her mouth, dark mucus stretching like elastic between her jowls.

"Mine," breathes the specter as she reaches a bony hand out of her cloak toward Vera.

Oblivious to the horror I'm seeing, the teacher shakes her head, and Vera only grows more animated.

"What about line 2? She says death *kindly* stopped for her. *Kindly*. Like he's doing her a favor."

Feathery, black wings burst from the shadow girl's back.

I glide back towards Vera. "Stop!" I want to scream at the specter, but it's the nightmare moment again—I have no voice. "Please," my thoughts cry out, "please someone make her stop!"

The darkness is nearly upon us when a flash of light explodes before me. The same shimmering effect and the unfurling of radiant wings, bursting with light, takes place. Blinded by the light, I cannot tell whether the shadow girl is still present. All I can hear is the teacher's voice.

"Vera, I think we get the picture. Let's move on to

another of Dickinson's poems."

Although the light still blinds me, I can hear Vera relax back into her seat with a sigh. The light fades, but I do not see Vera. I do not see the classroom at all. I am once again in total darkness.

I am worried for a while that I have lost Vera. Although I do not really know her, she is the one constant in my fractured existence. No matter how many times I get plunged into darkness, Vera is always there when I return.

While I wait in the darkness, I begin to wonder about her. Why is she the one I always see? Was she someone I knew in life but have forgotten? I don't remember most of my life. My death is the one thing that remains clear. Should I recognize Vera? She is not my sister Cecille; I remember that much. I had a sister and two parents, although they separated three years ago. Now I worry that perhaps the shimmering light didn't save Vera at all. Perhaps the darkness got to her too. Perhaps she is somewhere waiting in darkness just like me.

The darkness ends, and I find myself in a church, but it's not the church I once knew. Church was something my family used to do all the time before my parents separated. Every Sunday we'd march into Saint Isaac's during the entrance hymn and then book it out of there right after Communion.

St. Isaac's was old, long and narrow. The walls were white except for the inside of the alcoves, which were painted a bright blue. From our pew in the back, the priest always seemed so far away. It didn't make matters any better that his homilies made me feel like he was even farther away from me and my life. What did the words spewing from his mouth have to do with me and my problems?

The church I am in now is quite different from St. Isaac's. The walls and ceiling are exposed wood. Instead of the traditional long and narrow approach to the altar, the pews are arranged in a semicircle. Behind the altar are tall, narrow windows, through which I can see a grove of trees behind a small field. The ceiling lifts up high so that an enormous crucifix is hung over the altar. The figure of Christ is so imposing I can't decide whether to be frightened speechless or laugh nervously. There's no missing the Jesus in this church.

But there's someone else I want to see right now more than a giant crucifix. Vera. What happened to her after I left the classroom? Is she in this church, like she has been in every other episode of light?

I scan the congregation. Two pews ahead of me, a young girl reluctantly rises to her feet as the cantor begins the Alleluia. Her mousy brown hair is not pulled back in a ponytail, but I know it's Vera. I glide down the aisle to get a closer look. It's her all right, and she doesn't look very happy. She is alone.

The priest reads the Gospel, and I vaguely hear him say, "Ask, and it will be given to you; seek, and you will find; knock, and it will be opened to you."

My attention is focused on Vera. What is it that brings me out of the darkness and back to her time and time again? What is it I'm supposed to be seeing or doing?

The Gospel ends, and everyone sits. The priest begins his homily, and I'm not really listening to his words until I realize a tear is slowly rolling a path down Vera's left cheek. I remember being bored many times in church, but never bored to tears. My attention shifts to the priest. Something he is saying is making her cry.

"We must persevere. We must believe that God will answer our prayers. If we ask for help, God will respond. If we seek Him, we will find Him. If we knock, God will open the door for us."

19

I shake my head. "It's a lie!" I shout, but of course, no one hears me. "He's lying!" I try to shout again. "God doesn't answer our prayers. God doesn't hear us."

Through the windows behind the priest, I see the grove of trees, and from that grove, a dark fog oozes out between the trees. I hear the wind picking up outside, but the trees don't move. The darkness heading across the small field toward the church swirls itself into numerous funnel clouds. Each cloud then becomes a shadow of a cloaked figure, like the bony ghost girl I saw in the classroom. The priest continues, oblivious to the legion of specters gathering outside.

"Sometimes we think God doesn't hear us because we don't always get the answer we seek, but that doesn't mean He isn't listening. Like a parent caring for a child, God is concerned with what's best for us."

"No!" I scream again. I rise up from the pew. "No, it's not true! God doesn't care about what's best for us. He leaves us hurt! He abandons us!" Having unwittingly glided toward the altar, I turn now to face the congregation. Men and women placidly gaze at the priest or cast their eyes down to read their bulletins. Children fidget in their seats, eat Cheerios, or stare off into space. How can they just sit there? Don't they know the priest is telling them a pack of lies?

"God doesn't answer prayers." I'm right in front of the priest now. My face is inches from his, but he doesn't flinch. He's still talking, but I can't hear him. The shadows swirling outside the church windows roar loudly. I hear nothing other than them and my own screams of "You're lying! You're lying!"

I catch a glimpse of Vera still crying in her seat before everything goes black, and my memory is flooded with all the reasons I ended my own life.

Chapter Four

The first memory I recall is of my parents fighting. It's brief but painful. I was ten. Dad had just lost his job, and Mom was in denial about changing her spending habits. She'd bought me a new dress for Easter, and it was such a pretty shade of robin's egg blue that I was giddy with excitement. I couldn't wait until Easter to wear it, so I put it on right away and insisted on wearing it during dinner that night.

My dad scowled at me. "You'll ruin that dress before Easter."

"No, I won't." I grinned. "It's too pretty to be ruined."

We had spaghetti for dinner that night. The dress was doomed from the start. I cried when the meatball rolled off my plate and onto my pretty robin's egg blue dress, the red stain like a splat of blood on a summer sky.

"Don't worry, pumpkin," Mom said. "I'll get the stain out."

The dress was removed among a torrent of tears, and Mom ran straight down to the laundry room while I threw on an old pair of shorts and a t-shirt. Worried my dress was ruined for good, I snuck downstairs after my mother, eager to watch her work her magic on the stain, but I stopped at the top of the basement stairs when I heard my father's voice.

"What were you thinking, Lily?"

"I was thinking it was a pretty dress."

"But the money."

"It's for Easter, Martin."

"I don't care what it's for. You know we ain't got the money."

"It was on sale."

"On sale? Are you dumb or something?" Dad's voice

21

rose. "It doesn't matter if it's on sale. If we ain't got the money, we ain't got it."

"You'll find a new job soon."

"In this economy, it could be years."

"Stop being such a pessimist."

"Stop being such a dreamer!" A bang and resounding echo told me Dad had pounded his fist on something hard like the dryer. "You've got to face reality. We don't have money for fancy things anymore."

"You should learn to have hope, Martin."

"You should learn to think before you buy. And then letting her wear it to dinner! Now we can't even return it. It wouldn't have been so bad if you had just let her wear it on Easter. We could have kept the tags and returned it the next day. Now she's ruined it, and she won't be able to wear it at all."

I couldn't listen anymore. I ran up to my room. I didn't know which was worse—learning my dress was ruined or hearing the hatred in Dad's voice.

My next memory is more painful and much more recent than the first. It took place only one month before my death. I had just come home from school, and like I had done every day for the previous two weeks, I checked the mailbox. DePaul University's website said they mailed their acceptance letters in mid-March. It was now almost April.

The mailbox lid squeaked as I creaked it open. There were the usual piles of bills and junk mail, plus Mom's copy of *Midwestern Living*, but sandwiched in between all that was the one thin envelope I'd been waiting for. The return address had the logo for The Theatre School at DePaul University. A few curved strokes and a circle gave the impression of a happy person with arms spread wide. I smiled. That was exactly how I was feeling at the moment—I wanted to throw my arms open and shout to the world, "Watch out, everyone! Here I come, future Tony-winner Nanette Dunston!"

I dropped the rest of the mail on the front hall table and grabbed the letter opener from the junk drawer in the kitchen.

Upstairs in my room, I carefully sliced the envelope open. I didn't want to rush this perfect moment. It didn't bother me in the least that the envelope was so thin. I figured more information would arrive later. After all, I still had to wait to find out if I'd won an academic scholarship. Without financial assistance, there was no way I could attend. But money was a problem I would worry about later. This moment was a dream about to come true.

With trembling fingers, I pulled the letter from its envelope. I sat back on my bed and settled into the pillows behind me, unfolding the letter only after I'd taken a deep breath. Wanting to savor the moment, I read the letter aloud, "Dear Miss Dunston, Thank you for applying to The Theatre School at DePaul University. Although your application and your audition showed signs of promise, we regret to inform you that we are unable to accept you into the fall class." My eyes gazed over the rest of the letter quickly.

"No," I said aloud. "There must be some mistake." I flipped the letter over to see if anything had been written on the back. I think I half expected to find a handwritten April Fool's note. I peered inside the envelope. There was nothing else, just my printed rejection slip.

I walked downstairs, the letter in my right hand, the envelope in the other. No one else was home. For a minute, I paced the living room floor. What was I going to do? I hadn't even considered a possibility other than DePaul. Sure, the college counselor at school had told me to list some alternatives, but really I never thought they would be necessary. I'd planned on DePaul ever since my grandmother had taken me to see one of their plays back in middle school. How could they not have accepted me? My audition had gone well; my grades were good--mostly. My test scores were fine.

When the denial wore off, the anger set in. I wanted to scream, I wanted to cry. How could they have stolen my dream?

I grabbed my phone out of my bag, punched in Ally's name, and pounded up the stairs to my room.

"Hello?"

"Ally, you are not going to believe this." The story came out in sobs and whimpers. Ally was the right person to call. She always knew when to shut up and listen and when to offer advice. At first, she just listened, which gave me the chance to vent. I denounced DePaul for not knowing talent when they saw it. I declared that their entire faculty was a bunch of has-beens. I swore the kids who did make it were all of the cookie cutter variety and that they had no appreciation for unique talent.

I went on and on about the roles I'd had in our school musicals and plays, about the many leads I'd had and the solos I'd sung in choir. Then I began a litany of the performances I'd been involved in outside of school—the community theater gigs and the park district dance recitals. Finally, I chastised them for breaking a girl's heart. Didn't they know this was all I'd ever wanted? That I'd grown up admiring them and dreaming of this?

Ally let me cry, and when I calmed down, she said, "You've got to decide on your next step."

"There are no next steps. This was it."

"No, there's always another step. DePaul isn't the only school that offers a theatre program."

"But it's the only one I wanted to go to."

Ally ignored my comment. "What about Northwestern?

They have an awesome theater program."

"Too expensive," I said.

"What about a state school?"

"The closest is Northeastern Illinois. It doesn't have a theatre program."

"What about Columbia?"

"The one in New York?" I squished up my nose at that one. Ally knew I had to stay in state. I would have loved to study in New York, but my dad said there was no way I was leaving the state. For one thing, it meant paying room and board, something Dad refused to do. For another thing, he said he barely trusted me at home. How could he trust me hundreds of miles away?

"Not Columbia University, silly." Somehow Ally managed to tease me without making me mad. "Columbia College in Chicago. You know, downtown."

My nose remained scrunched. "Isn't that in a bad neighborhood?"

Ally laughed. She'd been a city girl until moving to the burbs at age eleven, so she always found my fear of the city amusing. "If you're going to be on Broadway, girl, you'll have to learn to navigate your way through a big city."

Ally did her best to encourage me, but the pain of being rejected by my dream school never quite wore off.

I try to push the third memory away—to keep it from replaying—but I can't. I'm forced to relive the worst. Yes, my parents' fighting and eventual separation caused a lot of pain, and the hurt of DePaul's rejection stung until my final breath. But it was an event three days before the end that took away any and all hope that God answered prayers.

Ally and I were on our way to the pick-up rehearsal for the spring play. The opening weekend's performances had gone so well, I'd almost forgotten my rejection letter. I was playing one of my dream roles, Abby Brewster, one of the maiden homicidal aunts in the farce *Arsenic and Old Lace*. The play is about a couple of sweet old ladies who think they are putting lonely old men out of their misery when they offer them poisoned wine. We'd sold-out crowds, and had even received two standing ovations.

On the way to the pick-up rehearsal the following Tuesday, Ally and I laughed over the mistake her fellow spotlight operator had made on opening night, lighting up stage right when he should have been on stage left, the effect being even more comical because his accidental lighting had caught one of the stagehands sneaking on stage to move a misplaced prop.

"You should have seen the look on Daniel's face when the spotlight hit him," Ally said, chuckling. "He wasn't just a deer in headlights; he looked like he was going to faint. There he was all in black with the bottle of elderberry wine in his hand, looking like a burglar trying to make off with the goods."

I slapped my hand against the steering wheel as I laughed. "Oh, I wish I had seen it."

"The look on his face was priceless. He looked like this." Ally made a face, and I turned to see her rendition of a shocked Daniel Peters caught on stage. Her eyes were opened so wide the whites showed all the way around her pupils. I laughed.

I shouldn't have laughed. I shouldn't even have looked at her while driving. I paid the ultimate price for sneaking that look at her. It only took a few seconds, but the time I took to turn my head was enough time for the car in front of me to slam on its brakes.

A spring rainstorm had made the road slick, and by the time I turned back to the road, I had to slam on the brakes. The old Civic didn't have anti-lock brakes, and in my panic, I forgot to pump the breaks until we were nearly on top of the gray minivan ahead of us. A few desperate pumps of the brakes and a quick twist of the steering wheel turned my car until Ally's side slammed into the minivan. The sounds of our screams, the crunching of the metal, the feeling of complete helplessness are things not even death can wipe from my memory.

I had been following too close. I had taken my eyes off the road. I had forgotten to pump the brakes.

And I had killed my best friend.

Chapter Five

The memories end, and I am back in Vera's church. The priest reads the final prayer, and I know the congregation will soon file out, but I can't wait until the final hymn is sung. I want out, and I want out now.

I don't want to see Vera anymore. I don't want to care what happens to her. Caring about other people just brings pain—Ally's death taught me that. I don't want to hear priests talk about God answering prayers. Where was He when I prayed to get into DePaul's Theater School? Where was He all those nights I heard my parents fight until I thought their voices would wear out? Where was He the night I killed my best friend?

Out. I have to get out of this church. I glide up the aisle toward an exit. Through the windows, I see the dark shadows continue to cross the field, but I don't care if they are out there to get me, or Vera, or anyone else. I want out. The shadows can take me if they want me.

At the exit, though, I stop. Not because I want to, but because I can't move any farther. It isn't the closed doors that stop me. I'm stopped a foot from them, but I simply can't move forward anymore.

I turn around. The recessional song has begun, and a few early birds walk toward me. I try to dodge them, but soon there are too many of them, and I can't get out of their way. It doesn't matter in the end, as a couple of them simply walk right through me. Vera walks down the aisle toward me. The desire to flee consumes me again. I fly out over the pews and head for the opposite side of church to use one of the other exits.

But when I get to the other side, I can't get past any of the other doorways either. In fact, as I near them, I feel an immediate tug behind me. The sensation doesn't make any sense. I have no body to be pulled, but I'm being yanked nonetheless. My very soul is dragged right through the pews, through the altar, and directly to Vera as if a strong magnet had suddenly been switched on.

The doors of the church open as parishioner after parishioner leaves. The dark shadows lurk in the background. They spin like funnel clouds, but none of them take on the figure of the shadow girl who visited Vera's English classroom. As the congregation spreads out across the parking lot, the shadowy clouds get pushed farther and farther back. Then I see them. Hundreds of little shimmers of light, like the one in the English classroom, hovering over the people. Some of them are small waves of bright joy. Others are closer in size to the one that came between me and the shadow in the classroom. On the far end of the parking lot, closest to where the darkness hovers, one shimmer of light unfurls its wings.

What are these things? Angels? The Holy Spirit?

I don't have time to wonder for long. I'm suddenly plunged into the darkness, but the anger of only a few minutes ago has vanished. I feel calm, relaxed. What did those shimmers of light do to me?

I follow Vera from class to class, looking for the shimmers of light, but I don't see any. If they are God's angels, why weren't they inside the church? Why only outside? And why don't I see any here in the high school now? Perhaps the shimmers only appear around those who believe. That would explain why there were so many of them near the parishioners, but wouldn't there be at least some at the high school?

As Vera moves through her school day, I look forward to English class. I am desperate to see another shimmer, and I'm convinced the one I saw near the English teacher will be there again. I wonder about this teacher, Ms. Kitchin—that's the name outside the classroom door. What caused her to have a shimmer unfurl its wings to protect her from the shadow girl?

Whatever the reason, I hope it happens again. I realize that on the two occasions I encountered them their presence left me calm and reassured. I long for that same sense of peace I experienced in the church parking lot.

If I still had a body, I would hold my breath as I enter the English classroom. As it is, I can only wait in breathless—and I mean literally, breathless—anticipation. Ms. Kitchin stands near the doorway, passing out slips of colored paper to the students as they enter. No shimmer hovers over her shoulder, and at first I'm disappointed. Then I remember that the shimmers only appeared when the shadowy clouds were around. Perhaps there's a connection. If the darkness rolls back in, then maybe the light will reappear.

Vera pulls a black slip from Ms. Kitchin's jar and sits in her usual desk. A few of the other students have black strips like Vera's, but most of them have red, blue, green, or white strips.

A boy I've never noticed before is sitting in the back corner. He looks much too old for this freshman English class. By the stubble on his chin, I'd guess he's at least a senior, but he could pass for college-aged. His hair is thick and wavy, and he wears a sweater that looks like it's straight out of the 1950s—v-neck with a button-down shirt underneath. Apparently, he likes retro looks. A quirky smile plays on his lips, and I'm thinking he could break a lot of hearts despite his throwback style. Yes, I definitely would've noticed him if he had been in the room before. Did he just move to the district? Or was he transferred here from another class?

The bell rings, and Ms. Kitchin starts class. The students break into groups based on the colored strip they pulled, and

Ms. Kitchin directs them to look at the poem on page 345. As the students move their desks, I watch the new boy, but he sits there, watching Ms. Kitchin. She ignores him. I wonder if she's even noticed there's a new kid in her class. He has no books. He doesn't even have a colored strip of paper.

I glide around the room to avoid the students as they move their desks. I know from my experience in the church that they can move right through me, but old habits die hard. Besides, it's too weird to know people can penetrate your space. When I shift to a new spot out of everyone's way, I realize the new boy is now looking at something behind me, and the smile that was playing on his lips before has broken into a full-on grin. I turn to see what has caused this amusement for him, but there's nothing behind me but an empty whiteboard. I turn back. He's still smiling, and his eyes are fixed on me. I figure there must be some mistake, so I glide a few feet to the right. His eyes follow me. I glide back to the left. His grin broadens even more.

"Do you think I can't see you?" he says.

Chapter Six

I do a 360, convinced someone must be behind me, but there's no one there. The students are all hunched over their textbooks, and Ms. Kitchin works off to the side with one of the groups.

The boy chuckles. "I'm talking to you, you know?"

I glide a foot closer. "You see me?"

"Yep."

"And you hear me?" What a ridiculous question. Obviously, he could hear me if he answered my first question, but the shock is almost too much to take.

"Of course." He's still grinning like a Cheshire cat.

"How? I screamed in church yesterday. I made a terrible scene, and no one saw or heard a thing. I even tried screaming in this room last week, and no one heard me."

"Oh, you were heard."

"By who? You?"

"Me, and a few others. Including One far more important than me."

I look around the room. Ms. Kitchin has moved to another group; otherwise, the class is still discussing their poems. None of them are aware of our conversation.

"But how can you see and hear me when none of them can?"

The boy leans forward against the desk, his hands clasped before him. "Because you and I are of the same kind."

I move another foot closer.

"Are you dead too?"

"In one sense of the word, yes I am."

"Then how come I haven't seen you here before?"

"I'm pretty sure you have seen me here before—at least once."

Now it's my turn to grin. "I'm sure I would have remembered someone like you being in this class." If I still had a body, my cheeks would be flaming. For a dead boy, he's pretty cute.

He leans back and folds his arms. "The truth is, I've been around here a lot longer than you have. Since you are new to all this, you probably didn't know what you were looking at. But I was here last Friday, and I'm sure you saw me. I might have just looked a little different to you that day."

Last Friday? I have no real sense of the days since I float in and out of darkness so often, but I know the day at church must have been Sunday, and my only memory before that was the day of the shadow…and the shimmer.

I step back. "You're not…" I search for a word to describe what I saw without making myself sound crazy. "You're not the…"

Thankfully, the boy saves me from my stumbling words. He unfolds his arms, and as he does so, he leans slightly forward and a pair of the most beautiful wings of shimmering light unfurl behind him.

"I don't understand," I whisper.

"You really are new, aren't you?"

"New to what? Who…what are you?"

"The same thing you are."

I shake my head. "I don't know what I am. I'm just a girl—*was* a girl. I was a girl who did horrible things…"

"Haven't we all?" he mutters.

"But I died. I took my own life."

"I figured as much."

"I thought that after I pulled the trigger I'd just be…gone. But I'm not. I'm still here, but no one sees me, no one hears me, but you. Please, I've been wandering in and out of darkness for days, or maybe weeks, I don't know, but if you know what's going on, please tell me." I move closer to him.

The boy's smile fades. "I think we'd better introduce ourselves first. I'm Warren."

"Nanette." I haven't said my name in so long it almost sounds foreign.

The boy nods. "A lovely name. Nice to meet you, Nanette. Welcome to Angelhood."

Time is so funny in Angelhood that I have no idea how much passes before I can gather my thoughts and reply, "Angelhood? Then I'm a..." The concept is so absurd I can't finish the thought.

"You're a Guardian, like me."

"A Guardian?"

The boy nods solemnly.

"I'm a Guardian, and this is Angelhood?" I look at the classroom of high school freshman around me.

"Well, technically, this is still Earth. You, however, are in *your* angelhood."

"As opposed to childhood?"

Warren chuckles. "Something like that."

"Let me get this straight. I'm a Guardian, and I'm in my angelhood, so what you're saying is that I'm a guardian angel."

Warren smiles. "Now we're cooking with gas."

"Huh?"

"Sorry, just an expression my grandfather used to say."

I try to think as the students around us push their desks back into rows. When they are settled, Ms. Kitchin begins a class discussion. Vera is in her usual seat. She looks bored.

"I'm Vera's guardian angel, aren't I?"

Warren nods.

"That's why I can never leave her. She's in every vision I have. I tried to leave her at church the other day, but I couldn't. I couldn't leave the building at all. And then I *had* to

34

leave the building. I was dragged out of the building because *she* was leaving. I *had* to be with her."

I look at Warren and get the impression he's waiting for me to figure out more.

"You said you're the same thing I am. That makes you someone's guardian angel, too." I look around the classroom. "You're Ms. Kitchin's guardian angel, aren't you?"

Warren smiles faintly. "Good to know you can still put two and two together."

"But we can't be the same. I don't have those wings." I watch as Warren tucks the shimmers of light behind him. "And I can see you clear as day. Heck, I thought you were a living, breathing student. Me? I don't have anything. I'm just a bundle of thoughts."

"Are you sure about that?"

He gestures toward the empty desk in front of him. I've been hovering over it for a while, but as I look down, a faint outline of my former body appears beneath me. I can almost see the jeans and t-shirt I died in. My ghostly arms have brought my barely discernible hands to lean on the top of Warren's desk.

"What's happening?"

"You're growing in grace," says Warren.

"What?"

"All angels start out with just their souls, just their thoughts, but an angelic version of your former body will grow in visibility as you grow in grace."

"Will *they* be able to see me?" I nod toward the living beings in the room who still continue their discussion of poetry, though I notice at least one student who's checking his cell phone under his desk.

"No, not unless they die and enter angelhood, too."

"How long does it take, this growing in visibility? When did you start looking like that?"

Warren sighs. "Who knows? Time isn't the same for us angels."

"But it must have been recently. Friday, when I saw you, you were just a shimmer of light with wings."

"That's what *you* saw, but that's only because you hadn't grown in grace enough to see me as I am. I suppose when you saw the 'darkness' as you call it, that you only saw a black shape, something like a cloud."

"Yes. Mostly. There was a face that formed, and a bony hand. Should I have seen something more?"

Warren grimaced. "Not yet. Don't worry about it. There are some things you really don't want to rush."

"But my body?"

"You want it back. I understand. Everyone misses their Earthly body. More of your former self will be visible as you continue to grow, but don't expect your body to return like it was before. That doesn't happen until the end of time. And even then, it depends on whether or not you make it to sainthood."

"Sainthood?" I nearly screech. Although I know the living beings can't hear us, I half expect them to turn around when my voice reaches an unearthly pitch.

"You didn't expect angelhood to be the end, did you? Don't get me wrong. Angelhood has its pleasures, but the ultimate goal is making it to sainthood."

"I'm no Mother Teresa."

Warren shakes his head. "You've got to stop thinking of your earthly definitions. Everyone who makes it into...well, heaven, as you would call it...is a saint."

"And what if I don't make it to sainthood? Am I stuck here forever?"

Warren bites his lip. For the first time, he seems unsure of his response. "Probably not."

"Well, then what?"

A bell rings and the students gather their books. Vera stands up and heads for the door. Already I feel the tug to follow her.

I look at Ms. Kitchin at the front of the room. She's preparing for the next class, and I realize Warren will be staying behind to protect her.

"Warren, what happens if I don't make it into sainthood?"

He gives me a half smile as my soul and wispy angelic body are pulled toward the door as Vera exits.

"I guess we'll have to save that for our next lesson, Nanette."

Chapter Seven

Out in the hallway, I'm barely aware of Vera maneuvering through the crowd. The ideas Warren has given me are so overwhelming. Part of me is in utter denial. How can I possibly be an angel? I killed myself. That's hardly angelic. I was a sinner. I did terrible things, although at the moment I can't remember all of them. I know I screamed at my parents when they said they were separating. I remember saying terribly hurtful things to both of them. I know I killed my best friend. And then there's my sister.

There's something about my sister I'm supposed to be remembering, but I can't.

A bright light zooms past me so fast it leaves a trail of shimmering stardust behind. Up ahead, the light blossoms into the image of a feisty, petite angel. She has long blond hair with a pink streak dyed through the right side, heavy dark eyeliner, and black fingernails. She wears a black tank top over ripped jeans and cargo boots. A tattoo of a Celtic cross adorns her upper arm. A pair of bright wings are tucked behind her.

She stands, arms crossed, and spreads her wings slightly in front of an older boy who's at least a foot taller than she is. He's wearing a varsity basketball jacket, and his hand, glittering with a fat class ring, presses against a blue locker.

Behind the tiny girl angel is another boy. He has darker skin and the beginning of a pathetic goatee growing on his chin. This younger boy keeps his eyes cast down and shoves some books into his open locker. The varsity boy is staring straight over the head of the tiny angel, his eyes glued to the goatee boy.

"Meet me in the usual place. Fifth period."

Goatee puts a book on the top shelf. "I don't know, man.

Maybe not today."

Varsity leans in. I am sure he has no idea his face is two inches above that of the angel. "What do you mean? You haven't bought in ages. You must've run out by now."

"I'm low on cash."

Even I can tell Goatee is lying. He's avoiding eye contact with Varsity like he's expecting them to shoot lasers.

Varsity glances up and down the hallway. I do the same. Vera is across the hall, twirling the combination on her own locker.

Varsity leans in another inch. "You've got the money. I've seen you working third shift at the station. Don't tell me you're not interested in having a good time anymore."

Goatee pauses as he pulls a folder out of his locker.

I glide to his other side.

He bites his lip.

The angel floats up, her face before Varsity's. Then she flips the tip of her wing. It hits a picture hanging on the inside of Goatee's locker. The picture—that of a pretty Latino girl with dark eyes and long wavy hair—flutters to the floor. Goatee stoops to pick it up, glancing at the picture before thrusting it into his pocket.

"I've got plenty of good times." Goatee smiles to himself, slams his locker shut, and heads down the hallway. Varsity is left standing with his mouth open. He rolls his eyes, pounds his open palm against the row of lockers, and heads in the other direction.

The angel turns around and follows Goatee, but not before winking at me as she passes.

"Score one for the good guys," she says.

I am shocked, but why should I be? If Warren could see me, surely other angels could too.

I glide over to Vera and watch her shuffle books in her locker. On the inside of her locker door are a mirror and several of those magnetic pink ribbons people put on their car bumpers.

A few feet to the left, another girl opens her locker and begins to put away books but not before glancing toward Vera. This girl is several inches taller than Vera. She looks at the mirror in her own locker as she adjusts the headband in her dishwater blond hair. I can only see her profile, but there is something familiar about her. Perhaps she's in some of Vera's classes.

Shifting the books in her arms, Vera puts a hand on her locker door to close it.

"You know someone with breast cancer?" says the dishwater blonde, pointing toward the pink ribbons in Vera's locker. Her voice is soft and a little sad. It, too, seems very familiar, but I can't put my finger on where I've seen or heard her.

"Knew," responds Vera without looking at her. "I *knew* someone with breast cancer." She closes her locker.

"Oh, God, I'm sorry, Vera."

"I'm sure you are, Cecille." Vera walks away without so much as a glance toward the girl, but I can't take my eyes off her.

Cecille...the name echoes through my very soul as the girl turns to watch Vera walk away. With her face turned toward me, I immediately recognize the pale blue eyes. How can this be? She was only twelve when I died. Can she really be a freshman in high school now? And look at how tall she's grown—at least six inches since I last saw her. Have two years really passed? They must have, for standing before me now is a girl who can only be my baby sister.

I want to stay and watch her, but Vera has moved down the hallway, and I am pulled away from the familiar dishwater blonde.

"Cecille!" I cry. "I'm so sorry." I want to sob, but angels

who don't have bodies also don't have tears.

Vera moves around the corner, and my world goes black again.

The memory rushes up before I can stop it.

It was three days after the car crash. Ally had died in the hospital a few hours after we arrived. I had walked out with only a few cuts and bruises.

Mom let me play hooky from school Wednesday and Thursday. Friday was the funeral. I was scheduled to perform in the second weekend of performances for the spring play, but Mr. Cardone, the theater director, called me Friday afternoon. It was school policy that you couldn't participate in extracurricular activities on days when you missed school, but as he put it, it was "probably for the best" that I not perform anyway. My understudy was perfectly capable, and the show would go on without me.

I was furious. How could I be replaced so easily? Acting was what I needed at that moment. I needed to be in another world. *This* world was too painful. I wanted to laugh at death, not wallow in its misery.

A hundred emotions swarmed me. I felt grief over the loss of my best friend, guilt over causing her death through my careless driving, anger over losing the part in the play, misery at having been rejected by DePaul, confused about what to do with the rest of my life, and utter despair that God ever answered prayers. Where was the joy in life?

I couldn't see any happiness. My future looked bleak and painful. My dad had just lost his job again, and Mom wasn't making much as a secretary. There was talk of my putting off college altogether to get a job. I was sick of listening to other seniors talk about their plans for the future. I was sick of never hearing good news.

I tore a page from my English notebook, scribbled a note

of explanation, and sat down on my bed. Next to the note, I laid Ally's obituary from the Pioneer Press. I didn't deserve to live.

No one was home. Cecille was having dinner at her friend Vicki's house, but Mom would be home soon. She would be the one to find me. I figured she'd be relieved. She was always complaining about how expensive my tastes were. Without me, there'd be more money for her and Cecille. Maybe this way Cecille could succeed where I failed. She could get the training she needed to be a world-class ballerina, and places like Julliard would clamor for her.

I heard a key in the door downstairs. Mom was home. I had to act fast. I pointed the gun at my head and pulled the trigger, my petite fingers straining to squeeze it. After the gun fired, my body flopped over onto my bed like a lifeless rag doll, my face pointing toward the door to my bedroom, as footsteps pounded up the stairs.

Then came the high-pitched scream. I could no longer see, but the scream was burned into my memory.

It wasn't my mother screaming. The scream was that of a twelve-year-old girl. Cecille—not my mother—had come home early.

Chapter Eight

The memory is so painful all I want to do is find Warren and figure out how to make the memories stop. I'm vaguely aware of following Vera out of class and through the hallway. She is back at her locker, and I scan the crowd, half hoping, half fearing, that Cecille will appear.

I can't believe how much she's changed. I know people say girls change a lot between middle school and high school, but it's amazing to see it all happen in what feels like a blink of an eye. How did she cope with seeing my death? What have the last two years been like for her?

Cecille doesn't visit her locker again, and Vera heads down the hall with a few new books and a reusable blue lunch bag.

The cafeteria is exactly as I remember it—too many overheated teenage bodies crammed around rectangular tables that can fold up and make way for a school dance at any moment. The room stinks of teenage sweat and overcooked beef stroganoff.

Vera takes her blue lunch bag to a corner table not far from the entrance. Another girl, tall and emaciated, sits in the middle of the table, munching on a pile of soggy cafeteria nachos. I've seen girls that look like this before. When I was a student here, a girl named Kallie routinely ate the worst crap in the cafeteria and then upchucked it all in the girls' bathroom later. Everyone knew she was bulimic, but no one cared about her enough to tell the counselors.

Vera sits at the far end and unpacks her lunch. She takes out neatly wrapped packages of food—a ham sandwich, two chocolate chip cookies that look homemade, an apple, and a sandwich bag full of pretzels. The last thing she pulls out is a water bottle.

43

At the opposite end, a boy and a girl dressed entirely in black, both with dark eyeliner and lipstick sit down. They don't have lunches. The boy pulls out a tablet and a stylus. The girl fiddles with a game on her phone. Periodically, the two talk to each other, but they are the only ones at this table who do.

I remember this table from high school. This was the loner table. People wanted nothing to do with it. It had the unfortunate position of being located right next to the garbage cans where everyone dumped their leftovers on the way out. If you wanted to be left alone by the rest of humanity, you need only sit at this table.

How did I end up being Vera's Guardian? I was by no means head cheerleader, but at least I skated by unbullied and I had a few friends. Okay, really only one good friend and a few so-so friends, but at least I had something. Vera has nothing. And even if I hadn't had Ally, I would have forced myself to find a friend, to sit somewhere, anywhere, other than at *this* table.

Warren said I'm supposed to be her Guardian, but I have no idea how to help her. I look around the cafeteria and wonder if there are other Guardians present. Vera seems safe for the moment, so I decide to stroll through the cafeteria. Maybe I can find that rocker chick angel I saw earlier. I want answers to my questions, and I probably won't see Warren again until English class tomorrow.

As I move around the cafeteria, I recognize a few of the upperclassmen who were freshmen and sophomores when I was here. Not surprisingly, Cathy Ringles still holds court with her fellow dance team members in the center of the room. I never quite got what made her so popular. She wasn't terribly pretty, but she had a knack for making people do what she said. There was some sad story about her older sister dying in a car accident, but I didn't think that gave anyone the right to be so pushy.

Off to the side is my old table, the theater geeks. I smile as I recognize some of the kids I knew from the drama club. Gregory Hicks has grown a beard, and Shana Peters has her hair pulled up in a ponytail, the bottom quarter of her head shaved. I wonder what skits they're working on now. Gregory always had a knack for incorporating pop culture into our acts.

The memories of what I've given up in life cause me to turn away and head down the aisle. A few tables down sit the group I liked to call the "wannabes." They thought they were popular, but didn't realize they weren't.

Across the room from them, a group of scowling kids slump around the stoner table. That was another table I avoided while I was alive. If any table in this cafeteria needs a Guardian angel or two or three, it's this one, but I don't see any wings or shimmering lights around.

I move along and pass by the jocks, the musicians, and the brainiacs. No sign of a Guardian anywhere. I begin to worry that I'll have to wait until tomorrow to get my questions answered.

At the loner table, Vera finishes up her ham sandwich and folds the aluminum foil neatly before putting it back in her bag. Undoubtedly, she will reuse the same piece of foil for tomorrow's sandwich.

"Finding any useful information?"

I whip around.

"Warren?"

"The sooner you get to know your Charge the better."

"My Charge?"

"Vera," Warren nods toward her before looking over the rest of the cafeteria.

"Warren, I don't think I can do this."

He studies my face for a moment before returning his

45

gaze to the students. "Oh, don't say that."

"But what I did...it's unforgivable. My sister—"

A new voice interrupts me. "Has it happened yet?"

On the other side of Warren stands the rocker chick angel who'd winked at me earlier. I wonder how long she's been there. Like Warren, she stands with her arms folded, surveying the crowd.

"Not yet," Warren replies. "Betsy, have you met Nanette?"

Betsy leans around Warren. "We met in the hall earlier."

I nod back at her. "What's going on? What are you both waiting for?"

"You asked earlier what would happen if a Guardian chooses not to try for sainthood. I'm afraid you're about to find out."

I look around the cafeteria. I had searched it carefully for anyone who might be a Guardian. If Warren's right, then someone in this room has to be an angel who has given up, but who?

The roar of a strong wind sounds from the hallway behind us. A dark shadow rushes toward the cafeteria. Its shape is like that of the shadow girl—a cloaked figure with a hood up. But this face is even more hideous. Unlike the shadow girl's slate gray skeletal face, this shadow has a crimson face of fire. Its eyes glow electric blue. As it approaches, it sucks air in and then expels it like it's breathing fire.

It turns its bright blue eyes toward us as it passes. Never before have I received such a look of pure hatred. It lets out a long rattling breath in our direction. A wave of heat passes over me.

Warren and Betsy stand firm, but I involuntarily glide behind Warren's shoulder.

As it glides through the cafeteria, I wonder where it will

stop. Where is the Guardian I didn't notice?

The stoner table. I want to glide closer to see, but there is no need.

A boy stands up from the table. "What?" he cries, his arms flung out wide, his eyes fixed on the fire-faced shadow before him. His angelic body is more translucent than my own. "What do you want?"

His voice is so loud that if he were still a living being, he would surely have had the attention of the entire cafeteria. As an angel, no one notices him. The others at the table remain talking or staring off into space.

"What's going on?" I whisper to Warren.

"He's a new angel, but not as new as you."

"Is that why he couldn't see me when I passed him?"

"He hasn't seen any of us," replies Betsy. "I don't think he's even seen our light." She shakes her head. "Never a good sign."

"But why? Why hasn't he seen any of us? I was able to see you eventually."

"Because you chose to see us," says Warren. "You were looking for help. You had some glimmer of hope in you. This guy won't even see the second chance he's been given."

Across the cafeteria, the former stoner screams, "Enough! I've had enough. Take me out of here."

Even from several tables away, I hear the shadow's hideous breathing. As it exhales, the air before it wavers like desert heat.

"Can't we do anything?" I ask.

"No," Warren says. "A Guardian can protect the living, but not another Guardian. The Guardian has to choose hope and love. He has to choose God."

"But the other day, in English class, you stood between me and the shadow."

Warren shakes his head, but his eyes remain focused on

the shadow across the room, which grows in size. "I wasn't protecting you. I was protecting Vera. A Guardian can help another Guardian protect her Charge if the Guardian asks for help, like you did. But a Guardian can't save another Guardian."

I look from Warren back to the shadow. It is now several feet taller than the former stoner-turned-Guardian who is still screaming.

"To hell with this life! To hell with this world!"

The fiery face inhales for what seems like an eternity. Then it hisses as it exhales, "This is your choice? You choose to reject what God has offered?"

"There is no God!" screams the stoner.

"So be it."

The shadow's jaw drops all the way to the floor. The elongated mouth is now a gaping hole of flame.

"Enter." The word comes from deep within the shadow.

The stoner steps forward and peers through the flames. The anger melts on his face as his mouth falls open. I can't see what he sees, but utter fear has replaced his bravado.

"No." He tries to back away, but a dozen tongues of fire leap from the shadow's open mouth and wrap themselves around him. For a moment, he writhes to break free, but his entire body catches fire, and his skin burns to a crisp, sizzling and crackling over the din of the cafeteria, before the tongues of flame pull him down into the shadow's mouth. The shadow collapses into itself, and the dark cloud disappears in a whirl that roars like a tornado and then ends abruptly.

There is nothing left of the boy who was a stoner.

The three of us Guardians watch silently. The students in the cafeteria chatter and eat, unaware of the horror we've just witnessed. My feet feel glued to the floor, my angelic body strangely numb, like a foot that has fallen asleep and is beginning to tingle. When I can finally move again, I turn to look at Betsy and Warren. Their faces are long and Betsy has her hand over her mouth, but it's a look more of sadness than of shock.

"Who was he supposed to be guarding?"

"Jason Arollo, who didn't start experimenting with drugs until a year ago when his parents divorced," Warren's eyes are on the stoner table as he speaks.

"What will happen to Jason now? Will the...will the...?"

"Will the shadows get him too?" Warren finishes my question. "Hopefully not. He must have prayed for help at some point in order to get a Guardian. Let's pray he keeps asking."

"How are things going with Ms. Kitchin?" Betsy asks. Her mournful eyes turn toward Warren. I get the sense she is eager to change the topic.

Warren sighs. "About the same as usual. Skating on the edge but always holding onto a thread of hope. How about yours?" Warren looks down at the tiny Guardian.

Betsy smiles a little. "Really good, actually. I think we're getting close."

"Really?" Warren returns the grin. "That's great. For both you and Luis."

Before I have a chance to ask what they are talking about, a bell rings and a hundred plastic chairs scrape across the cafeteria floor.

"There'll be a meeting tonight," says Betsy. "You going?"

Warren nods. "It would be a good time to bring the newbie too." He nods in my direction.

"Me? Bring me where? What meeting?"

Betsy glances at me and then looks up at Warren. "You're right. Will you make sure she gets there?"

Warren nods.

"See you tonight then." Betsy glides off among the teenagers. Vera has left her table, and I'm being pulled through the throng. Warren stays by my side.

"Warren, what meeting? What was Betsy talking about?"

"I'll explain later. Meet me outside the school at midnight."

"But what about Vera? I can't leave her." I gesture toward her. "I mean, literally, I can't leave her."

"As you grow in grace, you'll be able to leave your Charge when necessary. Some times are easier to leave than others. Even a new Guardian like you should be able to get away while she's sleeping. Just believe that it's possible, and you'll be able to meet me tonight."

"But where are we going?"

"I'll explain tonight."

Vera turns into a stairwell. I'm forced to follow her, but Warren remains in the hallway.

"You're an experienced Guardian. Can't you leave Ms. Kitchin and explain more now?"

Warren shakes his head. "Sixth period is a rough class for Ms. Kitchin. I'll see you at midnight."

"Wait!" I yell, but there's nothing I can do. Vera is spiraling her way up the stairs, and I float right over everyone's heads as Vera walks out on the second floor.

For the rest of the day, I try to forget both the horror of the cafeteria incident and the memory of my sister's scream. Instead, I focus on Vera. What can I do to protect her? She spends most of her class periods scrawling in her thorny heart notebook, but when I look over her shoulder, she's not writing down what the teacher is saying. She's writing poems. I read over her shoulder:

The numbness seeps through my veins.
I cannot deny it its course.
It will reach every corner,
It will pick through my brain.

Oh, this undeniable force!

Not bad for a freshman mimicking Emily Dickinson.

All day long, no one talks to Vera, and she says nothing unless called on by a teacher. The good news is I don't see any more shadows, which is especially good since I have no idea how to fight one off. When Warren protected Vera last Friday, he seemed to just spread his wings and the shadow vanished.

I look behind me, and I don't see any wings. I put my hands in front of me. My body seems to have grown in visibility a bit since this morning. How long until the wings follow?

When Betsy stood between the drug dealer and—what did Warren call Goatee guy? Oh yeah—Luis, Betsy's wings knocked a photo off his locker. Was that all it took? There has to be more to it than that.

Watching Vera, I feel completely helpless. How will I know how to protect her when the shadows reappear? And what exactly am I protecting her from? The same fate I witnessed in the cafeteria? That can't be right. Humans aren't just swallowed whole in the middle of their lives. I'm going to have a lot of questions for Warren tonight.

In the afternoon, Vera walks home. It takes about a half hour, which makes me think she'd qualify for the bus, but she's chosen to walk instead.

At home, a few attempts at homework are made, and then she heads to the kitchen. Like one of my previous episodes with her, I watch her make dinner—this time spaghetti—and then her dad comes home and the two of them eat silently.

After dinner, there are more attempts at homework, an unfunny sitcom on TV, and then she heads to her room to read a book. All in all, her life seems pretty boring. Is this why the Guardian who was a stoner wanted out? He was bored with following around a loser all day?

I shake my head. I have to stop thinking about Vera as being pathetic. Sure, she's made choices to isolate herself that I wouldn't have made, but she's a girl who obviously feels deeply. And she's not too bad with words. Surely, she must have something to offer the world.

As Vera climbs under her pink comforter, I realize I haven't been pulled into the darkness all day. I've managed to stay with Vera for longer than any of my previous episodes.

"Huh," I say aloud in the darkness of Vera's room. "Maybe there's hope for me yet."

Chapter Nine

By half past eleven, Vera is sound asleep. It's time to head out. At the door to her room, I stop and look back. It feels weird to leave her. She's been the one constant since my death. What if something happens to hear while I'm gone?

Warren said I could and should do this. Perhaps at this "meeting" I'll learn how to protect Vera from the shadows.

Stepping toward the hallway, I expect to be pulled back into Vera's room by the invisible force that ties my soul to hers, but I remember what Warren said. All I need to do is believe that it's possible. I take one last glance at Vera through the doorway and then move down the hall. Even though Warren told me I could do it, I am still amazed.

The house is completely quiet. I glide down the stairs, remembering how I'd tried sneaking out of my dad's house one weekend so I could head to a late movie. The stairs had betrayed me with their old-house creaking. One benefit of being an angel is you don't have to worry about making noise.

At the front door, I pause. How do I get out? I've been following Vera through doorways, but she isn't here now to open the door. I reach out my hand, but instead of grasping the knob, my fingers move right through it. That's when I remember I'm no longer bound by three-dimensional space.

Still, it feels weird to move through the door, so I close my eyes as I do it. The cool night air greets me. The street is quiet except for the rustling of an animal in a nearby tree. I head off toward the school. A few houses still have lights on. Flickering lights behind a curtain tell me someone is watching late night TV.

The high school is completely dark when I arrive. A lone car sits beneath a light in the parking lot. I peer in as I pass by. The car looks deserted. I move toward the front entrance. Am I supposed to meet Warren inside? I hope not. Even though I'm already dead, the idea of moving through a darkened, empty school makes me shiver.

I sit on the front steps. It gives me a good view of the front parking lot so I can watch for Warren. The marquee outside the school scrolls through a list of upcoming events (Soccer game @ home, 4:00 Thursday, Cross Country Invitational @ Maine North, Saturday 8:00 A.M.). Then it shows the time: 12:01 A.M.

I stand up and move toward the parking lot. Is this some kind of Guardian initiation prank?

"That marquee's always got the wrong time."

I jump at the sudden voice and spin around. Behind me, Warren grins mischievously.

"You scared me to death!"

"Technically, that's not possible."

"Seriously, that's not funny." If he were a living boy, I would have smacked him on the arm. "When did you get here?"

"Few seconds ago."

"How? I didn't see you come up."

"You've got a lot to learn, Nanette."

"Yeah, well, you've got a lot of questions to answer. Like where are we going? And what's this meeting all about? And how on Earth am I supposed to protect Vera from the shadows?"

Warren holds up his hand. "Whoa! One step at a time. To answer your first question, we're headed to Our Lady of Sorrows. Know it?"

I shake my head.

"It's a basilica in the city."

The city? Great! If Ally were around, she'd be laughing over the thought of me trying to find my way to this place.

"I don't even know what a basilica is."

Warren walks around the school. "It's a special kind of church. There are only three in the city. This one's in kind of a rough neighborhood."

"Wonderful. A rough neighborhood and it's nighttime."

Warren smiles. "No need to be afraid, little Nanette. Where we're going, no shadows dare enter."

"So how do we get there? If it's in the city, it'll take forever to walk."

"True. And your wings aren't really big enough for flying yet." Warren cranes his neck to look behind me.

"My wings?!" I try to look over my shoulder at my back. "Where?" Of course, I can't see anything, but that doesn't stop me from trying to get a good look and nearly spinning in circles to do it.

Warren laughs. "You're like a dog chasing its tail. Trust me. They're starting to grow. In the meantime, I'll have to help you. Here, take my hand." Warren holds out his left hand and unfurls his wings. Their brilliance lights our surroundings. I wonder if my hand will go right through his like it went through the doorknob, but it's surprisingly solid and warm. I'm suddenly reminded of how good it felt to hold my mother's hand as a child.

"Ready?" Warren looks at me.

I nod.

"Here we go."

Since my angelhood began, I've gotten use to the sensation of gliding—of moving without feeling the floor beneath you—but flying takes gliding to a whole new level. I feel even more weightless, and the speed at which we move reminds me of the freeway.

We fly through the suburbs in record time, the lights of the streetlamps blurring past us. Warren takes the path of least resistance, swerving up, over, down, or around depending on what is in our way. Before long, we enter the city. We pass stores, factories, renovated apartment buildings, large city parks, and empty lots. The beauty and the stillness of the night consume me, and for a while, I forget the many questions I need to ask Warren.

Before I can fully appreciate Warren's flying skills, we slow down in the middle of a poorer neighborhood. On one side of the street stand old apartment buildings with small weedy front yards. On the other side sit several two-flats with boarded-up windows. A small stretch of newer brick buildings look like condos, but the sidewalks are still cracked and the street is littered with fast food wrappers and plastic cups.

The church stands at an intersection. It's large and white with a tall bell tower to the left of its entrance. With expert skill, Warren brings us to a gentle stop, and we drop onto the cement sidewalk in front of the basilica. An old car with a thunderous bass zooms by. We walk up the wide stairs to the three dark doors of the church. Above them are three tall stained glass windows. Separating the doors, four gigantic ionic columns stretch up at least fifty feet.

We pass through the first set of heavy wooden doors only to find more doors a few feet inside. These are red with the letter S embossed over the letter M. I want to ask Warren what the letters mean, but beautiful singing from inside distracts me. An incredible choir is singing God's praises. I don't know the words of the song, but its beauty makes me want to jump right into the soprano section.

As we enter, I gasp at the grandeur of the church. I haven't had much experience with different types of churches. All I've known is my little old-fashioned church, and I hadn't been in that one much after my Confirmation. Then there was Vera's modern church with its semicircle shape and exposed wood beams.

This place, this basilica, seems enormous compared to either of them. The pews are filled with people. Correction, angels. Their wings are neatly tucked behind them as they bend their heads in prayer. My gaze leaves the angels and moves straight up. The ceiling is vaulted miles above us, with little squares of blue — purple? — set among white lines. In the center of each square is a white floral design. At least that's how it appears, but from so far below I can't really tell.

On the opposite end of the church is the largest white marble altar I've ever seen. It's not just a marble table like at my old church, but an entire, intricately carved backdrop that must be at least thirty feet wide and two stories high. The stark alabaster nature of the altar stands out against the golden walls behind it.

"Impressive, isn't it?" Warren whispers in my ear. I can barely hear him over the singing of the choir.

I nod. "What do we do now?"

"The communal prayers will start soon. We should take our seats." Warren nods to others as we pass them. He leads me up the center aisle about halfway before sliding into a pew where Betsy is already kneeling in prayer. Warren pulls out the kneeler in front of us and bows his head. I mimic his movements, but I feel like a complete hypocrite. The last time I was in a church, I screamed at the priest, called him a liar, and swore that God never answered prayers.

"Warren," I lean over and whisper, "I've got a hundred questions to ask you."

"Shh," he says.

"But—"

"Later."

For a time, I kneel there not knowing what to say or think and just letting the choir's song wash over me. At least the music is calming.

As the other angels pray, I make a mental list of the

questions I need to ask Warren. How do I protect Vera? How will I know when it's safe to leave her like he knows when he can leave Ms. Kitchin? How do I make my wings grow? He said the goal was to make it to sainthood, but what does that actually mean? I also want to ask him what happens at these meetings, but I'll find out soon enough.

As the choir starts its next song, I remember what I saw in the cafeteria. When that Guardian denounced God, the shadow consumed him. Why didn't the shadows get to me when I screamed at the priest in Vera's church? I shudder at the thought of all the shadows that were waiting outside. Then I remember that when I had followed Vera out I'd seen many shimmering lights. I know now that those were all angels, but they couldn't have been protecting me; Warren said Guardians couldn't protect other Guardians.

When the hymn ends, the angels stand. In front of the altar is the tallest angel I've ever seen, taller than any human I've ever seen. His wings are unfurled, and they stretch nearly fifteen feet across. His purple robes and shimmering wings stand out against the white marble and gold wall behind him.

"My fellow Guardians, we come here this evening to pray for the soul of Kevin Mason."

"Who?" I whisper to Warren.

"The Guardian we lost today."

I raise an eyebrow, but Warren ignores me. I don't understand why we are praying for a soul that has been lost. The angel at the front continues his prayers, and I make a note to ask Warren what the good of praying for Kevin could possibly be.

After the prayers end, the angels sit again.

"And now, I call forward the Assignments Committee to nominate a new Guardian for Jason Arollo."

A group of male and female angels enter from the left and stand before the head angel. Dressed in golden robes with their sizable wings tucked behind them, they stand in a row along the communion rail.

"Committee Members," the head angel addresses them in a loud voice, "have you chosen a nominee?"

"Yes," says a female angel in the center. "Brother Joshua, we nominate Elizabeth Wolf."

"Cause of death?"

"Overdose. Cocaine."

"And the condition of her soul?"

"Her soul has finished the first stage of purging. She is ready to see the light."

"And how do you know she will succeed where Kevin failed?"

The female angel pauses. A few of the golden-robed committee members sneak sidewise glances at each other.

"Elizabeth was pressured into trying cocaine by peers. Her death was a result of her first use of the drug. She is fully aware of the dangers Jason is putting himself into and the peer pressure he's facing."

Joshua, the head angel, looks thoughtful, then nods. "Any personal connections?"

"Elizabeth was friends with Jason's cousin. She has never met him, but we think she will recognize the name."

Joshua looks over the heads of the committee members. "Does the community of Guardians support the nomination of Elizabeth Wolf?"

"We do," is the resounding answer from the angels around me.

"And will you support Elizabeth as she endeavors to bring the light to Jason?"

"We will."

Then the head angel steps down to join the committee members and together they form a circle. In a loud voice, Joshua proclaims, "We call forth the soul of Elizabeth Wolf to be a Guardian of the People of God." A starburst explodes in the center of the circle, lighting up the face of every angel in the basilica. Instinctively, I throw up my hand to shield my eyes from the light. Then the ball of light dwindles down to a few feet in diameter. "Elizabeth Wolf, may you shine with the Light of the Lord, and may you bring His peace to your new Charge." The angels lift their hands, and the newest angel rises above the committee members' heads. She is simply a sparkling ball of light at this point, like she's made of the same thing as angel wings.

"Go with the grace of God."

"Amen." The answer, from every being present except me, resounds through the church.

Elizabeth's light dances above the committee members' heads. Like a toy that's been wound up, it shoots upward bouncing off the blue-purple squares of the vaulted ceiling and sending out bursts of light like a sparkler on the Fourth of July. The Guardians applaud, the choir busts into a joyful tune, and Warren, with his faced turned upward, smiles. The newest angel ricochets back and forth across the vaulted ceiling reminding me of a lightning bug I captured in a glass jar when I was ten.

I join the applause as some of the other Guardians shout their encouragement to their new peer. The sparkling soul of Elizabeth Wolf spins several times in the center of the church and then rushes toward the narrow stained glass windows above the doors. For the briefest moment, I fear she will shatter the glass, but in true angel style, she simply flies right through them.

As the applause dies, the Guardians turn to each other and chatter. I guess the meeting is over. I turn to Warren. "What happened to Elizabeth just now—is that what happened when I first became a Guardian?"

Warren takes his eyes off the stained glass windows. "It's

pretty much the same for everyone. Actually, as I recall, you spent a lot longer bouncing your way around up there. Didn't she, Betsy?"

"Oh, yeah." Betsy gives me a grin. "You took at least five minutes finding your way out of here. I thought we were going to have to draw you a map."

Warren laughs and nudges Betsy. "Could you imagine us all holding signs with arrows?" Warren mimics holding a poster above his head and gesturing wildly. "That way, Nanette! That way."

The two of them laugh at my expense, but I don't care. I'm too confused to be bothered by a little joke.

"How do I know you're not making that up? I don't remember being here before."

"Skeptical, aren't you?" Warren jokes. One look at my face tells him I'm tired of the jokes. He changes his tone. "Nobody remembers the beginning of their angelhood. It'd be like remembering your birth."

"Oh. Yeah, I guess some things are better forgotten." I'm about to ask if he and Betsy knew I would be at the same high school where they were guarding when a loud scream silences the Guardians in the church. Faces turn toward the entrance.

"Help!" a voice calls from outside. "Help!" Someone pounds on the heavy wooden door. "He's going to kill us!"

Chapter Ten

Immediately, the Guardians rush for the door. I'm swept away with the crowd. Within moments, the entire collection of Guardians passes through the entrance and forms a protective half-circle around a teenage girl who is banging her first against the dark wooden doors.

"Help!" she screams again. At her feet lies a second girl. This one presses her hand against her side. From the scarlet stain widening on her shirt, I can tell she's been hurt. The reason for her pain is standing at the foot of the first step: a frantic boy pointing a gun at the two girls.

"Shut up, Theresa. Just shut up!" the boy yells.

The Guardians tighten their circle around the girls, and I can't help thinking that if the boy could only see the multitude of angels, he'd be frightened enough to leave.

Theresa stops pounding on the door long enough to face the boy. "Leave us, Tyrone!"

"Not till she pays up."

"She don't owe you nuthin'."

"Like hell she doesn't. Where's my money, Kia? I want my money." Tyrone moves up one step. My attention is on his gun. It isn't too different from the handgun I'd used to take my own life. Seeing the gun in the hands of such a young boy makes me want to vomit. The realization of how quickly I'd ended my own life and the memory of my sister finding me makes me want to rush forward and snatch the gun from him, but I know my hands would slide right through it. Out of the corner of my eye, I see Joshua, the head angel from the ceremony, slip back into the church. How can he leave at a time like this?

"She don't got your money," Theresa screams.

"Don't lie to me, girl. I'll take you out too."

Theresa turns back to the church door and pounds again.

"Who do you think's gonna help you? Nobody cares about you. Couple of dumb chicks." Tyrone eases up a couple more steps.

Theresa screams again. A heavy door creaks inside the church. Tyrone stops on the fourth concrete step.

"Hello?" Theresa cries. "Help, please! My friend's been shot!"

A crack of light appears under the door. Then the scrape of locks being opened. Tyrone backs down a step. The wooden door creaks open, and a sliver of light falls on the church steps. As it grows, the shadow of a tall man falls over Kia, who lies slumped on the concrete.

Tyrone bolts. Theresa stands in awe of the tall man now silhouetted in the doorframe. At first his face is in the shadows, but then he steps forward into the faint light from the nearby streetlamp. Joshua is dressed in a priest's collar, his wings nowhere to be seen.

The Guardians watch quietly. I whisper to Warren, "Can the girls see him?"

He nods. "Only the most powerful of angels can become visible to the living."

Joshua takes one look at Kia and then Theresa. "We need to get your friend some help. Hold the door."

A stunned Theresa holds the door as the angel comes forward, cradles Kia in his massive arms, and carries her inside. The Guardians all turn to follow them. At the rate Tyrone was running, he must be a couple blocks away already.

Inside the church, the disguised head angel places Kia on the nearest pew. The poor girl groans as her head rests against the old wooden pew. Her eyes close, and her hand slips off her gunshot wound.

"Come," Joshua speaks to Theresa. "Put your hand here.

Keep pressure on it. I'll get help."

Theresa does as she's told. "But…" She looks toward the church door.

"You'll be safe here," Joshua says, and he takes off for the back of church. The Guardians close ranks around the two girls.

Kneeling by Kia's side, Theresa begins to weep. "Kia, you can't leave me, girl. You gotta stay strong. You can't leave me like this." Theresa looks around. To her, the church must appear empty. She takes in her surroundings: the many side chapels with their statues, candles, and small altars; the paintings of Jesus's life hanging between each side chapel; the vaulted ceiling of blue squares high above her head; and the crimson red doors embossed with the S over the M. Stifling her tears, Theresa turns to the left, and her eyes stop on a painting of Jesus's crucifixion. On his left, a criminal hangs on another cross. In front of Jesus are a disciple and his mother. Dressed in her oft-depicted blue robes, his mother keeps her face turned toward Him as she watches her son die.

"Oh God," Theresa sobs the prayer. "Please don't let her die."

The banging of a door closing causes Theresa to flinch. A man I've never seen before enters from the far side of the church. He is short and bald and carries a black bag. He's wrapped in a navy blue bathrobe. When he sees Theresa's head peering over the back of a pew, he races toward her.

"What's happened?" he asks as soon as he sees Kia lying across the pew.

"She's been shot."

From the pocket of his navy bathrobe, the man pulls a phone.

"Who are you?" Theresa asks as the man dials three quick numbers.

"I'm Father David. Don't worry. We'll get your friend

64

some help." He puts the phone to his ear.

"What about the other priest?"

"What other priest?" He looks at Theresa, then focuses on his call. "Yes? Hello? Our Lady of Sorrows Basilica, 3121 West Jackson." He pauses.

Theresa rises from her kneeling position but keeps both hands on Kia. Her fingers are now stained with blood. "The other priest. The really tall one."

Father David lifts an eyebrow, but says into the phone, "A girl's been shot. She's bleeding terribly."

Theresa continues, "The one who went to get you. The one in black with the…" She lifts one bloodstained hand to gesture. "The collar."

Father David doesn't seem to hear her. "She's in the church right now. How'd she get here? I don't know. Just send an ambulance quickly." He listens again. A few more words are exchanged between the priest and the 9-1-1 operator as Theresa looks around the church.

"We should get going," Warren says to me.

"Now?" I ask.

"She'll be fine. They'll both be fine."

I look around and notice that the Guardians have started to go their own ways and the priest has headed to the front door. He pushes his way through the red doors, and I can hear him fiddling with the heavy wooden doors that lead outside.

Betsy leans toward Warren. "Meet back at the school?"

"We should have a little time before morning comes. Matthew coming too?"

Betsy looks over at a male Guardian who is standing near the doors and talking to pretty female Guardian with a pixie haircut. "Yeah, I'm sure he'll want to come."

Father David walks back into the church and switches off his phone. "How did you get in? The doors are locked."

"I told you," Theresa says. "The other priest. Where is he? Tyrone woulda killed us if he hadn't opened the door."

Father David steps closer. "My dear, I don't know who let you in this church, but I'm the only priest here tonight."

"I don't understand. He said he went to get help. How did you know I was here if he didn't come get you?"

"I was in bed when my phone rang. The voice said someone was hurt, and I was needed in the front of the basilica right away. Just to bring my phone and hurry. Nothing else. I figured it was a prank, but I thought I'd better check it out."

In the distance, sirens wail.

"Come on." Warren nudges me. "Help is here now." Warren grabs my hand and pulls me through the church doors. I get only a quick glimpse of the ambulance as it pulls up in front of the church—lights flashing, siren dying—before we're flying through the city again.

I'm really angry and frustrated, but I'm not sure why. Perhaps it's because I was given this job of being someone's Guardian and I never asked for it. When I put a gun to my head, it's not like I thought, "Oh great, now I can go watch gangbangers put guns to other kids' heads," or, "Yippee, now I get to follow around a girl whose life is worse than my own."

Next to me, Warren's wings are unfurled as he skillfully skims us over the tops of Korean dry cleaners, Italian restaurants, and bungalow homes. I'm angry at him, too. Why doesn't he ever answer my questions? It's always "rush here," "rush there." I haven't fallen into the darkness in a while, but in some ways I feel more in the dark now than I did before.

Then there's my anger at that kid Tyrone. He looked like he was only fifteen. What was he thinking, shooting that girl? If Theresa ratted him out, he'd be arrested, and what would his life be like then? Then again, what did I really know about any of those gang kids? They weren't a part of my life in suburbia. My only experience with gangs was watching them in movies. For all I know, maybe someone had put a gun to *Tyrone's* head trying to get money out of him.

When we get back to the high school, Warren flies us up to the rooftop. I'd been up there a few times my freshman year. Some of the science classes cultivate a garden up there; I have a vague memory of planting tomatoes with my biology class.

Betsy is already there, as well as the Guardian she'd indicated back at the church. Matthew looks like he's in his early twenties, and the way his t-shirt is stretched over his torso, I can tell he worked out a lot when he was alive. The two of them sit on a bench near the herb garden, their heads bent together. They look up when Warren and I land.

"Nanette, meet Matthew."

I nod in his direction, my arms crossed. I want answers, not more angels.

Matthew stands up and offers me his seat. I shake my head to indicate I'd rather stand.

"So what's your story, Nanette?" he asks.

"My story?"

"Yeah, every Guardian's got a story. I spent my childhood being beat up by an alcoholic father. In high school I doped on steroids so I could return the favor, only to end up addicted and just as drunk as he was. So what's your poison? Booze? Cocaine?"

"I don't have one," I say, but I'm beginning to wonder if every Guardian was a soul who had missed out on a 12-step program somewhere.

"She's a lifer, like me," says Warren.

"Oh." Matthew's eyes grow wide.

"What are you talking about?" I say. "What do you mean

I'm a 'lifer'?"

Betsy lifts her head. "That's just Warren's way of saying you committed suicide."

Warren turns away and takes the empty bench spot.

"Wait a second. Warren, you killed yourself?" He seems so cheerful all the time. I couldn't imagine him being that depressed.

Matthew answers for Warren. "Not only did he kill himself. He did it very dramatically, too. Hanging like a limp rag—"

"Enough, Matthew." It's the first time I've seen Warren mad, and even if I were the size of Matthew, I don't think I would've wanted a spot on Warren's bad side. The death glare from his eyes is enough to shrink the strongest of men.

Matthew turns his attention back to me. "So who are you in charge of?"

"I'm guarding a girl named Vera."

"Vera who?"

"I don't know."

"You're supposed to be guarding her, and you don't even know her last name?"

"Listen," I seethe. "I don't even know what I'm doing here. The last thing I remember—really remember—is the high-pitched scream from my baby sister when she walked in and found me with half my head blown off. Since then everything's been crazy. I spend half my time in darkness. When I can see at all, I'm following around a girl I'd never met in my life. There are dark shadows lurking everywhere, pulling souls into an oblivion I can only imagine, and I've got other dead people telling me I'm supposed to be guarding this girl from the shadows. Which, by the way, I have no idea how to do!" I pace in front of the herb garden. "I don't even know *why* I'd want to guard this girl. Her life's worse than my own." I want to take back the last two sentences, but my anger and frustration have taken control. I'm on a roll now and can't stop myself. "And it's not like she's very nice. My sister asked her a simple question in the hallway today, and Vera just brushed her off."

Warren and Betsy stand up from the bench.

"Sister?" Warren asks. "Did you say you saw your sister?"

All three of the Guardians look at me, concern in their eyes.

"Yeah, I saw my sister today. Her locker's just two down from Vera's. Cecille asked her if she knew someone with breast cancer. The inside of Vera's locker is covered with those magnetic pink ribbons."

"This sister," says Betsy, "she's the same one who saw you die?"

"I've only got the one...*had*...I only had one."

I walk to the edge of the roof garden. I can see over the roofs of houses for several blocks. Somewhere beyond these ranches and split-level homes is a blue farm-style house where my baby sister is sleeping.

From the other side of the tomato plants, I hear Betsy whisper to Warren, "Did the committee make a mistake?"

"I don't know," Warren says. "I've never heard of this happening before."

"Never heard of what?" I head back to their end of the roof garden.

Warren looks like he's about to speak but stops.

Betsy speaks instead. "When Guardians are assigned, they are given a Charge that they can relate to. Someone who has a similar problem. Matthew's sins are alcohol and drug related so he's guarding the assistant football coach who's pushing steroids on his players. Someone who'd died from anorexia would guard a soul with an eating disorder."

Two of the scenes I'd experienced between periods of

darkness flash before me. The scene in the bathroom of Vera with the kitchen knife, and the scene in the classroom when she'd argued that Emily Dickinson had had a death wish. "And I'm guarding Vera because she's thinking of committing suicide."

"Yes," Warren says simply.

"So what's the mistake you're so worried about?"

Matthew continues where Betsy left off. "There's another consideration the committee makes when they assign Guardians to Charges. They want you to feel some connection to your Charge, but they don't want you to be so connected that you can't see clearly, that you get distracted." Matthew pauses and looks down at the rooftop garden as if he could see straight through it to the classrooms below. "This is your high school, isn't it?"

"Yeah, so what?"

Matthew turns to Warren. "I might have thought it was a mistake if this hadn't been her school. You know, if maybe her family moved, and her sister happened to end up at the same school as her Charge. But to put her back in the same high school she just left…"

"Maybe it was an oversight," Warren suggests. "Maybe they didn't realize—"

"Of course, they realized," Betsy says. "They know exactly what they're doing."

"Then why?" asks Matthew.

I can't take them talking about me like I'm not here. "Guys. It doesn't matter. So what if I saw my sister? Listen, I'm not going to get distracted by her. I don't even want to see her. Seeing her reminds me of what I did to her. Besides, I don't plan on staying a Guardian for long."

As soon as I say it, the wind howls, causing the herbs to tremble in their pots. The rush of the wind behind me makes me turn around. A dark shadow flies up over the edge of the rooftop garden. But this isn't any old shadow. It's the one with the crimson face of fire and the electric blue eyes, which right now are burning holes right through me.

Chapter Eleven

The other Guardians' wings unfurl immediately. In the moonlight, their shimmer is iridescent. Warren said they could not protect me, but I think their reaction is involuntary.

"Keep away from her, Belphagor," Warren shouts over the howling wind.

The shadow exhales its fiery breath as it passes through the chain link guardrail that follows the perimeter of the garden.

"You can't save her, Warren." Belphagor's breath warms the chilly night air. His electric blue eyes gaze at each Guardian in turn. "None of you can."

"Watch what you say, Nanette." Betsy's voice trembles behind me. The wind circles into a vortex and nearly swallows her words.

"She must choose for herself." Belphagor turns to me. His bright blue eyes have no pupils. "Tell me, is this what you thought you'd get when you ended your earthly life?"

I shake my head. "I thought I'd find peace."

The shadow sweeps closer, the heat radiating from him. When he speaks again, his voice is calm, seductive. "I can bring you peace."

I'm mesmerized by his presence. "Peace..." My voice echoes.

Betsy throws her tiny angel form in front of me. "Nanette, think about you're saying." Her dark-lined eyes brim with tears. She throws the pink streak in her hair behind her ear. "You don't want this. If you want peace, this isn't the way to get it."

Belphagor sways in the wind behind her.

I turn to Warren. "You said angelhood wasn't the end. You said there was something else...sainthood."

Warren rushes forward. "Yes, and it will bring you far more peace than the shadows ever could."

"He lies!" Belphagor shouts. "I can offer you immediate relief from your pain. You'll never have to remember what you did on Earth again."

I'd love to forget certain things—the rejection from DePaul, the car accident that killed my best friend—but do I want to forget *everything*?

I face Warren again. "Tell me what I need to do to get to sainthood."

The nostrils on Belphagor's hooked nose flare. He begins to back away.

I look in Warren's hazel eyes. "I don't want to forget everything."

The shadow hisses. "I'll be back. Your Charge has already picked out the day she'll die. It's only a matter of time. Of course, I can return sooner…" His breath rattles. "…if you tire of trying to save a worthless soul." Belphagor flies over the precipice, taking the howling wind with him.

Behind me, the others let out a collective sigh.

"I thought we were going to lose you like we did Kevin." Betsy's wobbly legs lower her shakily onto the bench.

"Look, I don't want what Kevin got. I just need another way out. What do I have to do?"

Warren runs a hand through his mop of wavy hair. "You need to protect Vera."

"So I'm stuck with her for the rest of her life or until she commits suicide? Which, according to Belphagor, is going to be sooner rather than later."

"Some Guardians do stay with their Charges until the end."

"And for others?"

"It's different for every Guardian," Matthew says. "You're assigned to your Charge for as long as she needs you.

In your case, you're on suicide watch. That means you're with her until the danger of suicide no longer exists—until she truly sees what a gift she'd be throwing away if she took her own life."

"So my job is just to keep the shadows away until that happens?"

"Actually, it's a little harder than that." Matthew rubs his brow like he's trying to erase a headache.

"How much harder?"

Warren continues the explanation. "You're the one who needs to help Vera understand what a gift her life is."

I laugh out loud. "You're kidding."

My comment is met with three somber faces.

"How am I supposed to do that? *My* life wasn't much of a gift. I certainly don't see how hers is. It's way worse than mine."

Betsy shifts uncomfortably on the wooden bench. "Nanette, that's kind of the whole point. In our angelhood, we're each asked to see how we took our lives for granted and then help another soul avoid the same mistakes we made. I OD'd the first time I tried crack. Now I'm trying to help Luis see that he doesn't need the crap he's been buying."

I thought of the boy Betsy had guarded in the hallway earlier. Her wing had knocked a picture of a girl off his locker while his dealer was looking to make a sale.

"You're using a girl, aren't you?" I ask Betsy. "Today, in the hallway, you knocked that picture down on purpose, so he'd see her and think of her instead of the drugs."

Betsy gives me a Cheshire grin. "I prayed for a way to distract Luis, and God sent Maria. She won't spend a second on Luis if she thinks he's using."

"But how can I help Vera if I don't have my wings yet? She can't hear me, or see me. I can't even flick a photo off a locker."

"Your wings will grow in," says Warren. "In the meantime, there are other ways. We can teach you."

The eastern edge of the sky glows a faint pink now. It blurs up into the blue night sky, pushing the darkness back. Morning will come soon. What will the new day bring? The night has certainly been eventful.

The other Guardians watch me, waiting for me to say something next. It looks like the journey through angelhood is going to be a long road. Finally, I say, "So how do I start?"

It is agreed that Warren will give me lessons on Guardianship during English class since we know we'll be spending that time together anyway. If necessary, the others can join us at night whenever they're able to leave their Charges. Apparently, growing one's wings is something best done with the help of others.

Before we leave the school roof, the Guardians advise me to learn as much as I can about Vera. If I'm going to help her see her life as a gift, I'm going to have to see it that way as well.

Learning about Vera turns out to be more difficult than expected. I am barely able to stay out of the darkness the next morning. Perhaps it's seeing how lonely she is. Or maybe it's the glimpse I catch of my sister in the school hallway, but I fall in and out of darkness the way I used to fall in and out of naps on the living room couch while Dad watched football on Sunday afternoons.

I'm startled when Warren nudges me. Vera is in English class, and I'm leaning against the bulletin board covered with posters explaining the different types of figurative language. I stand upright. Warren is at my side.

"How long have I been in English?"

"About two minutes."

"The darkness...I..."

"Don't worry about it," Warren says. "A lot of new Guardians slip into the darkness now and then. Besides, you had a busy night." He winks.

I grimace and look around. Ms. Kitchin reads from a book of poetry. Vera's thorny heart journal is tucked inside her textbook.

"So time for my first lesson, right?"

"First, tell me what you've learned about Vera so far."

I sigh. Great, I've barely been out of the darkness this morning. I rub my forehead and try to remember the previous episodes. "She has no friends. She eats alone in the cafeteria at a table where only the biggest losers sit. She makes dinner for her dad each night, but the two of them never talk." I shrug my shoulders. "I guess that's it." Warren waits for me to say more. "Well, she also thinks Emily Dickinson was suicidal."

Warren sits on the edge of an empty desk behind Vera. "You're forgetting something."

"What? That she has Ms. Kitchin for an English teacher? You already knew that."

"Noooo," Warren says. "You told me last night about her locker."

"The pink ribbons?"

Warren nods.

"Okay, so I guess she knows someone with breast cancer." I stop and think again about what Vera had said. "*Knew*," I correct myself. "Somebody she knew died of breast cancer."

"And you said she and her father eat alone every night."

"Oh God," I slump back against the bulletin board again. "Her mom died of breast cancer. Is that why she's suicidal?"

"Think about your own suicide. Was it one thing that brought you to the point of putting a bullet through your head?"

I shake my head. "No, it was many things."

"You need to figure out what those other things are in Vera's life, too."

"How is that going to help?"

"The more you know about the evils Vera has seen as well as the joys she's experienced, the better you'll be able to nudge her in the direction of remembering the good."

"And how exactly am I supposed to nudge her? People walk right through me. My wings haven't even grown in yet, remember? I can't do that cool knock-the-photo-off-the-locker trick that Betsy did. Besides, what good would that do? Here, Vera. Here's a picture of your mom. Remember how good times were back when she was alive, before she got all sick with cancer and her hair fell out from the chemo and the doctors chopped her boobs off?" I clamp my mouth shut. Even I'm disturbed by how far I can go.

Warren ignores my grotesque imagery. "Your wings will come with time. You have to grow in grace first. Actually, believe it or not, your wings grew a little last night when you decided against going with Belphagor."

"What's up with that guy, anyway? He's way spookier than the shadow girl who came here last week."

"There are many shadows. All of them are souls who chose the darkness instead of the light. Basically, they're fallen angels. Belphagor is one of the seven 'princes of hell.' His job is to go after Guardians who despair. The other shadow you saw here last week is Tamesis. We don't know much about her, but we suspect she probably went to school here. She seems to like haunting the lonely souls of this building, like she's got some vendetta against them."

"What do I do to keep her from coming back?"

"Start seeing the good in the world. Then help Vera see it, too."

I look around the classroom. Ms. Kitchin has passed out

a worksheet full of questions. A couple students groan when she's says they are due tomorrow. Ms. Kitchin frowns but says nothing.

"Right now, I'm seeing a classroom full of bored teenagers, and a teacher who wishes she were anywhere but here. What's so good about that?"

"Come here," Warren pulls me to the windows. "Look outside. Don't you see anything wonderful out there?"

Outside a gentle wind rustles the leaves that have fallen to the ground. Two squirrels chase each other around a tree trunk. Heavy clouds linger overhead, obscuring the sun from view.

"Not really," I reply. "It looks like a dull fall day to me."

Warren sits on the edge of the heater. "I'm going to let you in on a little secret, Nanette. There's always something wonderful out there, even when you can't see it right away."

I snort. "Right!" I shake my head at Warren. "Have you always been Mister Positive? Haven't you ever felt like God's abandoned you?"

Warren studied the dark clouds outside. "I used to, but then I realized I was wrong. You see those clouds out there?" He points outside, and I nod, like he's asking the dumbest question ever.

"Tell me, Nanette, has the sun disappeared?"

"Yes," I say.

"No, I mean, does it still exist? Sure, you can't see it behind the clouds, but is it still there, on the other side of the clouds?"

"Of course."

Warren nods. "God is like that. He's still there, still warming the earth, still spreading his goodness. Sometimes we can't see Him because all the clouds are in our way, but that doesn't mean He isn't there, shining away."

He gives me a moment to ponder this, then adds, "Now

tell me something you see out there that makes today worth living."

I look at Warren. Part of me wants to remind him we're dead, but he's not looking at me. He's looking out the window with the most peaceful look on his face. I turn back to the scene outside the school. "The leaves," I say. "Especially that tree over there, on the edge of the parking lot. The way half of the leaves are bright red while the others are pumpkin gold. That tree is worth seeing."

Warren turns to me and smiles. "Good. What else?"

Through the window, I see a car parallel parking across the street from the school. The tires crush the leaves the homeowner had raked off the lawn.

"That pile of leaves. Some kid would probably love jumping into them."

"Does it remind you of memories from your own life?"

Warren's question is all I need to slip back into the darkness.

Chapter Twelve

The darkness lasts only a moment before a memory takes its place. It is an old memory. I was only seven. Cecille was just a baby. Mom pushed her in a stroller, and Dad held my hand. We had driven down to the lakefront and parked our car near Lincoln Park Zoo. First, we walked along the path, but Mom said there were too many runners, too many bicyclists. I was fine with that. I wanted to get into the zoo.

The leaves crunched under my feet. The wind whipped at my face, but I didn't care. Once we got inside the zoo, we found there weren't many animals out, but that didn't bother me either. I chased blowing leaves across the asphalt paths while my parents sat on a bench and Cecille slept in the stroller. Nothing exceptional happened that day. Except — we were together as a family, and that was enough.

The memory ends as quickly as it began. When I come out of the darkness, Warren is waiting for me.

"You remembered something from your life." It's more of a statement than a question, but I nod anyway.

"A happy time." Again, not a question. How does he know? "Now use that memory."

I look at him like he's told me to speak Finnish. "Use a memory?"

Warren looks around the room. "We'll start with something small. You won't be able to do the big things, like move your wings, until you've grown more in grace." He smiles at me. "But you can make the wind blow."

"Huh?"

Surely, Warren has lost it. He points to a jock who is seated to Vera and resting his head against his hand. From one angle, it looks like he might be working on his assignment, but he's actually asleep.

"See that pencil on the edge of Rodger's desk. Blow it right over the edge."

"What? I can't do that. I don't have any breath anymore."

"Not like humans have, but you do have angelbreath." Warren pulls me into the aisle next to Rodger. On the opposite side of Rodger is Vera, who has flipped her assignment sheet over and is composing her own poem on the back.

"Stand right here." Warren moves me by my shoulders. "Then lean down and blow. You'll make the pencil roll right off the desk."

I roll my eyes, but he looks so excited about me trying this, that I follow his instructions. Bending down, I close my eyes, and exhale like I'm blowing out birthday candles. When I open my eyes, the pencil's still lying there.

"I told you I couldn't do it."

Warren shakes his head. "You've got to think about that memory. The good one. The one that made you smile."

Smile? Had I actually smiled?

"How's this going to help Vera?"

"Just try it already."

I bend down again and stare at the pencil. It's not much of a pencil—pretty stubby, well-chewed, and only a little eraser. It shouldn't take much of a breeze to get that thing moving.

"Think about that memory. What was it the fall leaves reminded you of?"

Family. That's what the crunch of fall leaves reminds me of. I close my eyes and picture myself chasing the whirling leaves around the zoo. From her seat on the bench, Mom yells at me not to wander too far. She's sitting next to Dad and rocking Cecille's stroller back and forth. For the moment, I am happy.

I hold onto the happiness, and as I push the tunnel of breath through my lips, I imagine I'm a kid blowing burnt orange leaves across the asphalt path.

The soft clatter of compressed wood on linoleum makes me open my eyes. The sound has the same effect on Rodger. Dazed, he looks around suddenly like he's trying to figure out if someone called his name.

I pass through his desk so that I'm standing in the aisle between him and Vera. The stubby, chewed-up pencil lies across a crack in the old linoleum floor. I look up at Warren.

"Did you —"

Warren smiles. "That was all you."

For the first time in forever, I'm excited. Then the truly unexpected happens. Vera sees Rodger staring at his assignment and lifting up his pile of texts and spirals to see if the pencil's rolled underneath. Vera bends down, picks up the pencil, and places it on Rodger's desk.

For a moment, the big oaf looks at it like he's never seen a pencil before. Then he turns and smiles at Vera. "Thanks." He might not be the brightest crayon in the box, but his smile is warm, and Vera's cheeks flush a little at the attention. In my mental checklist, I add "Never had a boyfriend" to the list of Vera's problems.

For the rest of class, Warren makes me imagine happy moments and blow other small objects — paper clips, scraps of paper — around the room. Sometimes it is easy; other times all I can remember are the times my parents fought, or the rejection letter from DePaul, or the sound of Ally's scream right before our car slammed into that minivan.

Exhaling wasn't hard when I was alive, but it's exhausting as a Guardian.

"It'll get easier," Warren says, but I find it difficult to believe. I'm actually glad when the bell rings, and I have to follow Vera to her next class while Warren stays behind to guard Ms. Kitchin.

"Keep trying to remember the good," Warren says as Vera stands up to leave. "And see if you can help Vera do the same."

I don't get how blowing a pencil or a piece of paper off a desk is going to do any good, but I decide to play along. It's the only way my angelhood will conclude with anything other than a very unhappy, very fiery ending.

While Vera takes notes in geometry, I try to think of happier times in my life. The problem is that every happy time seems to be paired with an unhappy time. I remember how excited I was when I got my first role in a high school play, the mayor's daughter in *The Music Man* my freshman year. But as soon as that memory fades, I remember losing the part of Laurey in Oklahoma the next year, and getting the part of Ado Annie instead. It was still a big part in the play, especially for a sophomore, but I'd had my heart set on Laurey.

Then I think about my eighth birthday party, the last one I had in the old house. My mom had invited all my friends from school and the neighborhood, and we played silly games like pin the tail on Barney until our sides hurt from laughing. But that only reminds me of my fifteenth birthday when my parents were so busy fighting over who got to take me out to dinner that neither of them bothered to ask *me* what *I* wanted to do for my birthday.

I called Ally the night before my birthday and complained about my parents being complete morons. The next morning, when I arrived at school, Ally had decorated my locker with a million comedy and tragedy faces cut from construction paper, and purple curled ribbons hanging like tiny streamers in a cascade. Taped to the outside was an envelope. Inside the envelope were two tickets to the local theater's production of *Wicked*. I had begged my parents to get us tickets, but Dad had already said we didn't have money for "foo-foo" stuff like that. Theater wasn't "foo foo" to me. It was my future—something my dad didn't want to believe. He wanted me to focus on a "stable career," something that had a good 401k plan and stock options.

As I look back on the memory, my vision focuses on the theatre faces Ally had taped all over my locker. Those side-by-side comedy and tragedy faces summed up life, didn't they? The tragedy exists right alongside the comedy. My parents may not have asked what I wanted for my birthday, but my best friend knew without even having to ask.

Friends, I realize. They were what made life worth living. I look at Vera sitting in geometry class. Mr. Gallagher has asked the students to compare their answers with a partner, but Vera sits there alone. Everyone around her has partnered up. I look to see if there's a Sleeping Beauty for me to wake up by blowing his pencil right off the desk, but there's none in this class. Everyone is alert and working with a partner. Everyone except for Vera, of course. She stares at her paper and writes words in the margins: *sharp angles dig into my skin, wretched numbers no one cares about, one is a very lonely number, even zero is better than one.*

The wind howls in the hallway. I don't even need to look toward the door to know what's coming. I'm losing Vera to the darkness, and if I don't do something fast, it will settle in her soul. There is no Warren to help me this time, but I know my little wind-blowing trick isn't enough to blow away a shadow if it enters the room. I need help, but how? From where?

I look around the room. None of the students notice Vera, alone in the back corner. The window next to her is open a crack, probably the teacher's way of airing the teen sweat out of the classroom. Vera continues to scrawl verses in the margin of her paper. Two aisles over, Mr. Gallagher discusses the problem with a wrestling jock and his buddy. Indignation fills me. Isn't it the teacher's job to make sure every student stays on task? Why hasn't he noticed Vera's alone?

In the doorway, the shadow swirls into formation. It is Tamesis, the shadow girl from last week. I glide toward the teacher. I must make him look at Vera. I try to tug on his shirt, but as I expect, my hand passes right through him. Angelbreath is the only tool I have.

I head back to Vera. On the windowsill next to her is a pile of math worksheets. The breeze through the window is gentle, barely ruffling the top sheet. I take in the biggest breath I can and blow on the papers. Nothing happens. Are papers harder to move than pencils?

Then I remember Warren's advice. I have to think of something happy, something that made my life worth living. I glance at Tamesis. Her gray, gaunt face gazes over the room until her sunken eyes rest on Vera. The teacher continues to work with the jocks. I need him to care about Vera like my theater teacher Mr. Cardone cared about me and my performances. He was the one who pushed me to take my acting to the next level.

Looking at Mr. Gallagher, I remember the kindness of Mr. Cardone, and then I turn to the pile of papers and with my breath, I command them to dance before me. The worksheets fly off the windowsill in beautifully curving arcs. I blow again, and they dance over the heads of the students, gliding and curling this way and that. Vera looks up in wonder as the ballet in sheets of white plays out before her. Out of the corner of my eye, I see the shadow halt.

Likewise, the rest of the students stop working. It doesn't take much to distract teenagers.

"Whoa! What happened there?" cries one of the stoners.

"That was freaky," says another. "The window's barely open."

Mr. Gallagher sighs. "It's only a gust of wind, people." He moves to pick up the worksheets, and a preppy girl from the front row hops up to help him.

Vera smiles as the last of the worksheets see-saw floats down to her desk. Mr. Gallagher takes it from her. "Excuse me, Ms. Lavoy, I'm sure you won't mind if I hang on to that assignment until tomorrow."

Vera shakes her head and looks down at her worksheet. Mr. Gallagher takes the paper and adds it to the ones Miss Goody Two Shoes from the front row has collected. He pounds the stack of papers against the windowsill to straighten them.

"Ms. Lavoy, have you discussed your answers with anyone yet?"

Vera's voice is small when she responds. "No."

"Ms. Anderson, discuss problem #12 with Ms. Lavoy."

Ms. Goody Two-Shoes pops up from her front row seat and heads back toward Vera. I can see Vera is uncomfortable, but the Anderson girl jumps right into a discussion, and I relax as Tamesis glides out of the room.

Chapter Thirteen

After geometry class, I decide that getting Vera a friend is priority number one. If I'm going to keep Vera from suicidal thoughts, then she needs a friend to be there for her. Like I had Ally before...I push the images from the car accident out of my mind.

At lunch, I make it my mission to get Vera to talk with the bulimic girl at her table. Maybe I can save two souls at the same time. The girls sit three chairs apart at the same table with the techy kids lost in their gadgets at the other end.

First, I try blowing one of Vera's aluminum foil wrappers over to the bulimic girl, hoping she'll pick it up and hand it back to Vera. No such luck. The bulimic girl just waves it off the table. Vera has to get up and move around the cafeteria table to retrieve it.

When Ms. Eats-and-Pukes finishes her soggy fries with cheese sauce and takes out some homework, I try blowing her pencil down the table, so Vera will have to stop it. Good girl that she is, Vera does stop the pencil, but Eats-and-Pukes doesn't even say thank you when Vera hands it back.

I'm exhausted again. I feel myself slip into darkness just to get a rest.

"All right, what else have you got?" I ask Warren the next day in English class. "The angelbreath trick works to a certain extent, but I'm going to need more."

"Did you think of other happy moments from your life?"

I nod. I'd thought more about Mr. Cardone. He'd been so supportive when the rejection letter came, telling me every actor has to deal with disappointment and how not all actors were theater majors in college. There were other ways into the career. Matt Damon had been an English major, he'd said.

I had countered with, "Yeah, but Matt Damon and Ben Affleck also wrote an Oscar-winning screenplay to jumpstart their careers." I, on the other hand, had no hopes of being a writer.

I shove that last thought aside. *Think about Mr. Cardone's encouragement*, I tell myself. He was the one who had cast me as Emily in *Our Town*. He was the one who made me join the Forensics Team so I could compete in the Oral Interpretation rounds. I'd won my category several times.

"Yes," I say to Warren. "I've got some good memories to work with."

"Great." He claps his hands together. He is sitting on top of the windowsill looking at the freshmen, like a crow on a fence post peering at the corn growing. "Let's have you move something bigger today."

I tell him about my paper-blowing trick from geometry class.

"I was thinking of something more substantial. Something that requires using your hands instead of your breath."

"My hands?" I look down to examine them. They aren't as translucent as they once were and the edges are more defined, but they don't feel as solid as when I was alive. "I don't think my angel form is solidified enough." I peek over my shoulder. No wings that I can see.

Warren gives me the once over. "If you concentrate on a good memory and are truly thankful for that moment in your life, you'll be strong enough."

I'm doubtful, but ask, "So what do I move?"

Warren looks around the room again. "It can't be *too* big 'cause they'll notice and then the poor freshmen will start thinking the room is haunted. And it can't be loud either."

Ms. Kitchin has passed out a quiz, and the students are quietly selecting multiple-choice answers. Any noise would attract their attention. Some of them even turn their heads at the metallic slam of a locker in the hallway.

"I got it," Warren hops off the windowsill and heads for the door.

"Where are you going?"

"Out in the hallway." He waves at me to join him.

I take a look at Vera as I pass. She seems safe, but I'm worried about how far Warren is taking me. He may feel confident leaving Ms. Kitchin behind, but I'm not so sure about leaving Vera. I peer over her shoulder to get a look at the test before heading out into the hallway. She's near the end. I hope that means she's confident of her answers.

Warren stands by a locker outside the classroom. "I'm here a lot during passing periods, and I've seen this kid open his locker a hundred times. The combination is 17-6-23."

"Fascinating, Warren, but what's that have to do with me?"

"Open it. 17-6-23."

I realize his plan is perfect. The kids in the room won't be able to see me moving the lock, and if they hear me, it won't matter because they'll think it's the real owner opening it. The only problem would be if another person came down the hall. I look to my right and left. The coast is clear.

I reach out with my left hand to grab the lock, but my fingers go right through it.

"Think about those happy memories. If you're going to grow in grace, you've got to think about how grace has already worked for you."

I'm still not sure what Warren means by grace. I remember talking about it a bit in Religious Ed classes, but that was a long time ago—I'd quit as soon as I'd made my Confirmation. Now I wished I'd paid better attention when I had gone.

"Happy memory," I say the words out loud and try to

picture the time I'd won my first Forensics event. I had recited Shel Silverstein's poem "Sick," and the audience had laughed and cheered loudly at the end.

I reach out again, and my fingers curl around the back of the lock so that it is pulled up off the locker. My right hand reaches for the dial of the lock. I can almost feel the black knob under my fingers. *Now spin*, I think to myself.

I stare at the dial, but the numbers don't move. My fingers slip off the knob.

"Hold on to the memory," Warren whispers next to me. "Remember how you felt."

"Elated." The fingers of my right hand twitch, and the dial jiggles, but I can't get it to turn. I think about the moment my name was announced as the winner in the oral interpretation poetry category, and the dial spins one measly white marker to the right. I drop the lock in disgust. "Why is this so hard? I moved an entire stack of papers yesterday."

"Don't feel bad, Nanette. Moving something tiny can actually be harder than moving something big. It all depends on what you want to do with it. Think about when you were a little kid. When we're preschoolers, we can grab a big fat crayon and color wildly all over a page, but then we get older, the crayons get smaller, and we're expected to color inside the lines. Then you move on in school, and you trade your crayon for a pencil with a tiny point, and now you've got to make the pencil move just right to create twenty-six different letters of the alphabet." Warren leans against the row of lockers. "Guardians don't learn everything in a day, or two, or ten."

"It's like having to learn to write or read or ride a bike all over again." I bring my head down to rest on the locker in front of me. The metal creaks.

"See?" says Warren. "You just moved the locker. If you weren't formed enough as a Guardian yet, you wouldn't have made that locker squeak."

I lift my head up. Next to me, Warren has a gleam in his eye. I take a deep breath, think about the way Ally had decorated my locker for my birthday and grab hold of the lock again. Feeling confident, my right hand twists the dial, and I get one good twist around before my thoughts switch from the comedy and tragedy faces on my locker to the pink ribbons inside Vera's. Who would ever decorate Vera's locker for her birthday? Nobody.

My hand slips right through the dial.

"What happened?" Warren straightens up. "You were doing so well. Where did your thoughts go?"

"I was thinking about how my friend Ally decorated my locker for my birthday once, and then I thought about Vera. If you don't have friends, you don't have anyone to celebrate with, much less decorate your locker."

"You're going to have to start finding the good in Vera's life, too."

"But there is no good in her life."

"Then help her create good in her life. Get her involved. Get her some friends. Give her a reason to live. If you don't…"

Warren doesn't need to finish the sentence. I know what happens if Vera doesn't have a reason to live. It's exactly what I did when I felt I didn't have a reason to live. As if on cue, a strong breeze blows through the hallway. I don't even wait for the shadow to appear before I rush back into the classroom.

I expect to see Vera looking all depressed and suicidal, but she's actually looking rather interested in a conversation at the front of the room. Two students — one boy, one girl — stand in front of Ms. Kitchin's desk. Two quizzes are laid before them.

"You want to explain this?" Ms. Kitchin points at the

papers.

The girl is all wide-eyed innocence — too wide-eyed to be believable. I don't know who she thinks she's fooling. "What?"

"You have the exact same answers."

The boy mimics the girl's attempts at innocence. "We do? Did we get them all right?"

"No." Ms. Kitchin doesn't smile.

Behind me, Warren stands in the doorway, luminescent wings unfurled. On the other side of him swirls a faceless shadow like a tornado waiting to touch down.

"Well, we must have gotten a lot of them right," says the boy. "Karina always gets an A, so if we've both got the right answers, I must have done well, too."

"Not exactly." Ms. Kitchin points to the first question on each quiz. "You've got the same answers. Too bad you had different questions."

Karina and the boy bend over the teacher's desk to get a closer look.

"There are several versions of the test — same questions, different order."

The boy opens his mouth and then shuts it. The bell rings, and the boy starts to leave.

"You're not going anywhere — either of you," Ms. Kitchin says.

The rest of the students get up and leave. By sheer willpower, Warren seems to be pushing the shadow out. Over the chattering of the other students, I can't hear what Ms. Kitchin is saying to Karina and the boy, so I follow Vera out of the room but not all the way down the hallway. I stop near Warren, who is watching the shadow retreat.

"It came for Ms. Kitchin this time, didn't it?" I say.

Warren nods. "Kids who cheat and lie always depress her."

"You said you were a lifer, like me." I stop, not sure how to continue. "And Matthew said Guardians were assigned people with similar problems. Ms. Kitchin...she's struggling to find a reason to live, isn't she?"

Warren turns toward the room. He looks sadder than I've ever seen him before. Through the doorway, we see Karina crying and her friend sweating. Ms. Kitchin looks worn out.

"She's lonely, too." Warren's eyes are sad.

"So...what do you have to do? Find her some teacher friends?"

Warren shakes his head. "It's more complicated than that. She's got friends."

"A husband?"

"No...I mean, yeah, I'm sure she'd like one, but there's something else. I haven't figured it out yet." Warren looks at the students passing us in the hallway. "You'd better follow Vera. I sent the shadow out, but who knows when it will return."

I'm dying to ask Warren more about Ms. Kitchin. I never thought about adults being suicidal. What did they have to worry about? Especially someone like Ms. Kitchin. She doesn't have any family to worry about. She doesn't have to decide on a career. Adults have their whole lives figured out. They've been through the crazy, hormonal, bipolar adolescent years.

As I glide through the students to reach Vera at her locker, I think about Warren, too. I really know nothing about him, but something awful must have happened to make him become a lifer like me.

Up ahead, Betsy flies over the heads of the high school kids. Beneath her is her Charge, the goatee guy, and they're headed my way. I'm about to yell hi, when a cold, dark presence passes by me from the opposite direction. It's the same Varsity boy who was harassing Goatee the first time I met Betsy. My Guardian vision seems to be changing the way I see things. This time as I look at Varsity, I see a shadowy darkness that trails behind him, like a blurred action shot on a slow-speed shutter.

Goatee glances at Varsity, but he doesn't say anything. He heads straight to his locker and starts spinning the dial. Varsity rests his hand against a neighboring locker.

"It's about time we did business again, don't you think?"

Goatee looks Varsity right in the eye. "We won't be doing business anymore."

Varsity chuckles. "Now that's where I think you're wrong. You're one of my best customers, and everybody needs a pick-me-up now and then."

I expect Betsy to swoop down and work some magic with her wings at any moment, but she's still hovering in the air. Behind Varsity, the dark shadow moans, but a face struggles to form in the darkness.

"Not me," Goatee smiles. He slams his locker shut and starts to head off. He doesn't get more than two steps before Varsity slams him back into his locker.

"Betsy!" I yell up at her.

She holds up a finger to wait.

Varsity pushes his square-jawed face into Goatee's. "Listen, scum. We had a business deal. I provide the goods, and you provide the money."

"And what if I don't want the goods?"

"I still want your money."

"'Course you do. You got your own habit to support."

Varsity pulls his head back. "What are you talking about?"

"Please. Everyone knows you're juicing up before each match. Those hulking muscles don't come naturally."

Varsity slams him against the lockers again. People turn

to stare in the hallway. Vera closes her own locker and scuttles off to geometry. I want to follow her, but I can't leave Goatee alone when Betsy's doing nothing to help him.

I fly toward Goatee ready to muster what little Guardian power I have, but Betsy swoops down and pushes me away. "No," she says. "It's time. He's got to do this on his own."

"What are you saying, man?" Even from where I stand, I smell the rank teenage sweat oozing off Varsity.

"I'm saying you got your own problems to worry about, and a little less income from me is the least of your problems. A little bird told me there's already a video of you juicing up online. Didn't Northern offer you an athletic scholarship?"

The bell rings. Some students duck into nearby classrooms. The remaining stragglers are either on their way to lunch or don't care if they're late to class.

"Who posted the video?" growls Varsity.

"Beats me. The video was taken in the locker room. I don't hang out there. I just heard some kids talking about it in art class. Said the thing's going viral."

Varsity unclenches Goatee's black t-shirt. His eyes are wide. "If I'm going down, you're going down with me."

"What are you going to do? Try to prove you sold to me? You forget I've been clean for over a month now." Goatee smiles. One of the remaining kids in the hallway is the beautiful dark-haired girl from the photo in his locker. She walks up to him as Varsity slams his fist against the lockers and storms off. "If you hurry," Goatee calls, "you might be able to figure out who posted it and convince them to take it down." Varsity bolts down the hallway. The dark beauty wraps an arm around Goatee's waist.

"Everything all right, Luis?" she asks.

"Perfect," he responds, and the two head down the hallway.

I turn to Betsy. I thought she'd be happy, but tears stream

down her cheeks, making her black eyeliner smudge.

"Betsy, what's wrong?"

She shakes her head. "It's so beautiful." She doesn't look at me. Her eyes are transfixed on a spot down the hallway.

I try to see what she's looking at, but all I can see are Goatee and his girlfriend disappearing around a corner. "What? Them?"

"You can't see it, I'm sure."

"See what?"

"I never knew it would look like this."

"Betsy, what are you talking about?" The hallway is completely empty now, and I'm beginning to think Betsy is losing her mind.

She reaches out a hand to touch my arm. "I'm going home, Nanette."

"Home?"

"My job is over. Luis won't be messing around with drugs anymore."

"Are you saying you're no longer his Guardian?"

"That's exactly what I'm saying."

"So you're going—"

"Home." She takes two steps forward. "Tell Warren and Matthew I said good-bye."

"Wait. You're leaving right now?"

"Oh, Nanette. I can't wait for you to see this. It's...indescribable." She takes a few more steps forward, and I realize she's becoming smaller and more transparent. It's almost as if she's walking up an invisible staircase and shrinking at the same time.

"Betsy, wait!" I want to know how she did it. How did she get to sainthood?

"I'll see you soon, Nanette." Betsy is barely more than a shimmering light now. "Hurry home, if you can." Her voice echoes softly like the chime of a small bell. Her light curls up into a tiny golden ball. It's about to disappear completely when it suddenly bursts forth in a flash of light that blinds me for a moment. And then she's gone.

Chapter Fourteen

When I join Vera in geometry, she's working on a problem with Miss Goody Two-Shoes. I wish Betsy had stayed long enough to tell me what she'd seen. It must've been something amazing to have her rush off like that. More importantly, I want to know how she did it. Part of me wants to run over to Ms. Kitchin's and find Warren so we can talk, but I've already left Vera alone for too long.

Lunch is relatively uneventful. I can't figure out how to get Vera away from the loser table. The bulimic girl doesn't pay attention when I blow Vera's aluminum foil toward her. Vera just looks up at the ceiling like she's looking for a vent that's blowing on her before retrieving the foil herself. At the end of lunch, I grab hold of the bulimic girl's shoelace, and she trips getting up from the table, spilling greasy napkins and the remains of some nachos all over the floor. Vera sweeps around to help, but the bulimic girl doesn't even acknowledge her presence. I'll say this for Vera, either she's got a kind heart or she's simply grown used to picking up after her father all the time.

Class after class, I watch Vera doodle and scrawl verses in her thorny heart notebook. Some of her lines are quite lyrical even if they are darker than an Emily Dickinson poem about Death with a capital D. When she isn't writing, Vera has a novel or poetry book tucked inside her textbook. I suppose if I'd had no friends, I would've spent more time with my nose in a book, too. By the end of the day, I still have no idea how to help Vera make friends, but I feel hopeful. Goatee boy had said he'd been clean for over a month. Maybe that's all it takes—a month or two of Guarding. I could do that.

After the final bell rings, Vera packs up her bag at her

locker. She's getting ready to leave when a familiar face breezes past. Cecille. Her face is red, and her eyes puffy. I expect her to stop at her locker, but she heads straight for the girls' bathroom next door to Ms. Kitchin's room. For a moment I forget I'm dead and call out, "Cecille, what's wrong?" My baby sister was never a crier. She was Miss Mostly Sunny to my Miss Mostly Cloudy.

Without a thought for Vera, I follow Cecille into the girls' room. She plops her pile of books onto the counter and heads into a stall. Another girl washes her hands at the sink and then leaves. As soon as the bathroom door squeaks shut, Cecille lets out a wail and sobs. I stand on the other side of the stall door, my angelic hands almost solid, pressing against the pink painted metal. "Cecille," I whisper her name.

A strong wind roars through the building.

"What?" I cry in outrage. The shadows have scared me in the past, but this time I'm pissed. Why can't they leave us alone for a minute? I just want a minute to be with my sister, even if I can't do anything to comfort her. I rush out into the hallway.

The shadow swirls and roars its way toward Vera, who is pulling on her coat and lifting up her bag. I fly in front of her and cross my arms. Why is the shadow coming now? Vera's afternoon was relatively fine. Sure some of her poetry was dark, but she got an A on that history test last period. I stand between her and the shadow, hoping pure anger will be enough to keep it away. It zooms toward us and then flies over my head.

Ha! I think. *Take that, ya measly piece of evil.* Only the measly piece of evil doesn't seem to care. It heads straight for the girls' bathroom.

"Cecille!"

When I enter, the shadow swirls outside the stall where my baby sister sobs hysterically. I throw myself between the darkness and the stall door, my arms spread wide in place of the wings I haven't yet grown.

"Leave!" I yell at the darkness before me. "You can't have her!"

Within the depths of the shadow, the outline of a face forms in the darkness. It is Tamesis.

"Cecille!" I yell even though I know she can't hear me. I try to pound my fist on the stall to get her attention, but it slides right through. Warren's words echo in my head: "Think about those happy memories."

How am I supposed to think happy memories when there's a death shadow coming after my sister? I tune out Cecille's sobbing and the shadow's howling winds, and try to think of a good memory.

When Cecille was eleven, she learned to knit. Her first project was the longest, craziest, most colorful scarf I'd ever seen. She gave it to me for my birthday. Wearing it was the last thing I wanted to do, but one cold winter morning, I was running late to school and couldn't find my usual scarf, so I grabbed Cecille's. You would have thought the girl had won the lottery the way she smiled when she saw it wrapped a hundred times around my neck to keep it from dragging on the ground. That girl who gave so freely and was pleased so easily does not deserve to die.

Picturing the smile on her face, I pound again. "Cecille!" This time the stall door jiggles on its hinges. I hear Cecille swallow a sob.

"Hello? Is someone out there?"

Cecille unlatches the door and peers out. Of course, she sees no one even though I am right in front of her and the shadow hovers behind me.

Tamesis backs up a bit. It's as if the shadows feed off people's despair. When they hate their very existence, the shadow comes running. When there's a moment of hope, it backs off.

After looking to her right and left, Cecille eases out of her stall. "Great," she says. "Now I'm hearing things." She walks to a sink and, resting her palms on the cold ceramic edge, stares at her reflection in the mirror. I follow her; Tamesis remains where she is.

In the mirror, I see Cecille's pale blue eyes are puffy and red. "What is wrong with me? Why am I such a moron?" She drops her head and the tears return. Tamesis creeps closer.

Turning away from the mirror, I face the shadow. Her breath is warm, but not nearly as fiery as Belphagor's.

Tamesis opens her skeletal mouth. "Mine."

"No!" I scream. "You can't have her." A shadow coming for me is one thing; coming for my baby sister is another. I have to get my sister away from Tamesis, but there is nothing in this bathroom for me to blow over or move to distract her. Besides, she already thinks she's hearing things.

Tamesis moves closer. I back up against my sister, the shadow's putrid breath washing over me. "No!" I scream.

The door creaks open. My sister straightens up immediately. At first I think my scream must have been heard, but Ms. Kitchin calmly walks in. She looks perturbed, but the annoyance changes to concern as soon as she catches my sister wiping away tears.

"Cecille," Ms. Kitchin's voice is soft. "What is it?"

My baby sister shakes her head. "Nothing, Ms. Kitchin."

"Don't tell me that. You've clearly been crying."

For a moment, my sister looks like she's about to confess something horrible. Tamesis hisses.

"Just a bad grade on a test," says Cecille.

Ms. Kitchin tightens her lips like she's considering whether or not to believe my sister. It's obviously a lie. First of all, she doesn't get bad grades. And if she did, she would've accused the teacher of some mistake and gone down fighting before sobbing in the girls' room.

Ms. Kitchin reaches for some paper towels. "I have a feeling this is about more than grades."

Cecille wipes away a final tear. "No, just a bad test. That's all. I'm sure I'll make up my grade with the next one."

The face on the shadow has melted back into the darkness. Tamesis is only a swirling cloud of darkness now.

"You know, I think there's still someone in the counseling office—"

Cecille forces a smile on her face. "I'll be fine, Ms. Kitchin." She picks up the books she'd thrown on the counter and heads out. Ms. Kitchin reaches for more paper towels as I follow Cecille out.

Warren is waiting in the hallway. "What happened?"

"Tamesis came for my sister. You might want to head into the girls' room. Ms. Kitchin's still in there with the shadow." No sooner do I say this than Warren's Charge walks out, a stack of paper towels in her hand. I wait for the shadow to follow, but it doesn't come. By this time, Cecille is at her locker packing up her things.

"I think we're safe for now," Warren says.

"Thank God Ms. Kitchin walked in when she did."

"You can thank me too." Warren sounds slightly offended but he's smiling.

"What do you mean?"

"Ms. Kitchin wouldn't have gone to the bathroom in search of paper towels if I hadn't knocked over her open water bottle."

I peek into Ms. Kitchin's room. She's wiping the floor near her desk. "How'd you know I was in there?"

"I could hear your screams. The bathroom walls aren't that thick, and you were screaming bloody murder."

"You would too if your baby sister were being shadowed."

"I wouldn't know how that'd feel."

"No siblings?"

Warren shakes his head. "None that I know of. I was abandoned at a church when I was six days old."

A heavy metal door closes at the end of the hallway. Cecille has disappeared down the stairs.

"I'd better make sure she's safe."

"No."

"Warren, she's my sister."

"She's not your Charge, Nanette. That night on the rooftop we told you we thought the committee had made a mistake in placing you here. This is why. You're supposed to be guarding Vera, not your sister. You can't guard both of them at the same time."

"But she needs me."

"Vera needs you. Vera is the one who prayed for the protection of a Guardian."

"But my sister's attracting the same shadow now."

"Then she'd better start praying for a Guardian of her own."

Chapter Fifteen

I'm torn between flying after Cecille and chasing Vera home. How do I let my baby sister suffer? If a shadow is after her, then she's depressed enough that suicidal thoughts have entered her mind. I may have taken my own life, but I'm not gonna let Cecille take hers.

As I glide down the school stairs, I think about Vera. She prayed to receive a Guardian. Even though I find her life even sadder than my own, I don't think she deserves to die. Across the parking lot, Cecille gets into a car. The woman behind the wheel has to be my mom, but I hardly recognize her. Her face is pale, and her head's wrapped in a colorful scarf. I wonder what weird fashion trend she's following now.

Going after Cecille is tempting, but she'll be safe with Mom. Vera, on the other hand, is headed toward an empty home. Wishing my wings were fully grown, I glide down the street to Vera's house.

On this fall day, cars turn on their headlights as the sun slides its way to the horizon. Vera's house is dark except for a light in the upstairs bathroom. I've been a Guardian long enough that passing right through the front door doesn't faze me, but the moment I enter, a wall of darkness hits me. I've come to expect some times of emptiness when I've exhausted myself from using angelbreath, but this total darkness is oppressive with its heat and closeness. I try to move around, but I feel boxed in.

Time escapes me, and I see only snatches of scenes, brief glimpses of life.

A text message on Vera's phone: "Working late. Have dinner on your own."

Darkness.

A date circled on a calendar: Friday, November 2.

Darkness.

A kitchen knife pulled from its drawer. Dark blood dripping slowly onto blue bathroom tile.

Darkness.

Bandages pressed onto young skin. A huddled shape sobbing under a pink comforter.

Darkness.

The first time I'm pulled back into the light for any significant amount of time is English class. Vera looks relatively content. Ms. Kitchin leads the class in a Jeopardy-style review game. Based on the questions, the poetry unit test must be on the horizon. Something appears wrong with the classroom scene, and then it finally hits me that Warren isn't there.

My first concern is he's not there to answer my questions. I've come to depend on him, and I need his guidance.

Then I realize my problems might be much worse than just missing a training session. What if he's already passed on? Betsy left without saying good-bye to the others. I just happened to be there when she left. What if Warren finished his Guardianship and Ms. Kitchin is no longer a suicide threat?

The only other experienced angel currently at school is Matthew, and I haven't crossed paths with him since the meeting three nights ago. I assume he's always in the athletic department, and sports aren't exactly Vera's forte. There's the new angel Elizabeth Wolf, but she's still a glimmer of light hovering around Jason Arollo.

I decide to take my training into my own hands. Vera has just given a correct answer to Ms. Kitchin's latest question, and the dim-witted but sweet hunk next to her has given her a high-five. Vera lets him slap her hand, but I notice she winces at his pressure. She squeezes one hand against the upper part of her other arm, and I remember the cuts I saw last night.

I try not to think too hard about the fact that Vera has resorted to cutting as I glide out to the hallway. The coast is clear, so I practice turning some locks. At least I can work on something while I wait for Warren to show up.

Every once in a while, I stop because a kid wanders down the hall, but I manage to turn the dial in both directions and stop at the numbers I want. The only hard part comes when I remember my sister being chased by a death shadow. To keep my mind off it, I focus on happy memories from my own life. Maybe it's because of the game going on inside the classroom that I think of all the games I played as a kid: Ghost in the Graveyard, Heads Up Seven Up, Silent Ball, and Red Rover. As long as my memories are fun ones, I can spin the lock in either direction.

A cheer erupts from inside Ms. Kitchin's room. I glide through the wall to see Vera's team congratulating each other. Mr. Beefy even slaps Vera on the back. Another wince.

"All right, settle down, everyone."

"Ms. Kitchin," a boy from the front row calls, "what's our prize?"

"Hopefully, a good grade on tomorrow's test."

"Awww," moans the boy and a few others join him.

Ms. Kitchin picks up a stack of papers. "Before the bell rings, I want to pass back your poetry writing assignments. There are some really good ones. I hope you submit your work to our school's literary magazine." As Ms. Kitchin passes out the assignments, she continues to talk about the school magazine.

I tune her out as soon as Vera gets her poem back. There's a giant A+ at the top of the page. In neat cursive handwriting, Ms. Kitchin has written, "What a beautifully haunting poem, Vera! Please submit this to the magazine."

Vera pulls the page close. With her left arm, she seems to

be shielding it from anyone else's view. She stares at Ms. Kitchin's words, her eyes scanning them repeatedly, then she quickly folds the page and stuffs it into the pocket of her binder.

The bells rings, and Vera dashes out of her seat.

"Vera," Ms. Kitchin calls, but Vera books it down the hall faster than I've ever seen her move. The binder is tossed into her locker along with books from her morning classes. Then she takes out one new book, geometry, and closes her locker. She hesitates, reopens the door and pulls out the binder before slamming the locker shut and twirling the lock.

I can't quite figure out what the look on her face means. She appears confused one moment, like she's looking for an answer, and then angry the next.

As Mr. Gallagher walks the class through proof after proof, I try to figure out what my next move should be. I need to help Vera see the good in life. She needs to feel that the good in her life outweighs the bad. This A+ is the first good thing I've seen in her life, but she seems upset by it. I can't figure it out. Who would be upset about getting an A?

In the middle of class, Vera opens her binder and pulls her poem out of the pocket. Behind her pile of books, she sneaks another peek at Ms. Kitchin's comment. She doesn't seem angry anymore, just a bit confused. She bites her lip, then stuffs the poem back in the pocket.

Maybe Ms. Kitchin's suggestion frightens her. I remember the first time I auditioned for a play. It was freshman year, the play was *The Music Man*, and I never expected to get more than a tiny part, probably just a townsperson — if I was lucky, maybe one of the pick-a-little ladies. When the callback list was posted and I was asked to read for Zaneeta Shinn, the mayor's daughter, I almost couldn't go through with it. I was convinced there had to be some sort of mistake. Maybe that's how Vera feels. Maybe she thinks Ms. Kitchin pities her and wrote the compliment to boost her self-esteem.

By the time geometry class ends, I have a plan. I'm going to convince Vera to submit her poem to the literary magazine. Unfortunately, I haven't a clue how to do it.

Lunch is the usual disaster. Vera sits alone at the end of the loser table while the bulimic girl wolfs down something that looks like a cross between tacos and a burnt thin crust pizza. The techy kids pay more attention to their gadgets than their food. I roam the cafeteria trying to figure out where other writer geeks might hang out. From my days at the school, I seem to remember that they were usually a mix of kids who did things like newspaper and yearbook. A few of them even crossed over into my beloved drama club since we were always looking for people to write skits. My greatest wish would be to get Vera on the staff of the literary magazine. Then maybe she'd make some friends, too.

One step at a time, I tell myself. Let's get her poem published. Maybe then she'll gain enough confidence to join the staff.

At one table, I find a redheaded girl who is dividing up a stack of neon-green flyers. I hear her say the name of the literary magazine, and I glide a little closer.

"If each of us hangs up five of these in every wing, we should have the place covered," the redhead tells her friends.

"I'll take the math hall," says one of the guys.

"I've got foreign language."

"History," claims another.

I peek over their shoulders. As I expected, the flyers are for the literary magazine. I need to get one of those under Vera's nose. I wish I still had my body. If I were still alive, I could easily talk these kids into giving me one of their flyers, or at least sneak one off their table.

When lunch ends, I follow Vera to her next class and try

to think of other ways to get her involved in school. Maybe she could join the newspaper too.

During biology, I leave Vera while she's working on dissecting a starfish. The hallways are mostly empty, but I'm not interested in people. I look instead for the neon-green flyers for the literary magazine. The staff has done a good job plastering the hallways with them. I head toward the hall where Vera has her locker. There's a neon green flyer taped to the wall fifteen feet away.

After waiting for a teacher to carry a coffee mug into his empty classroom, I think about the fun I had in drama club and rip the flyer from the wall. As I try to carry the flyer down the empty hallway, my thoughts sidetrack twice and the flyer slips from my grasp, fluttering to the floor. But each time, I think of a particular performance I enjoyed or the applause I heard and I pick the flyer back up and carry it farther down the hallway. You would think the stickiness of the tape would help the flyer stick to me, but apparently tape doesn't mean anything to an angel's body. With some concentration, I manage to get the neon green flyer pinned on Vera's locker. She can't miss it now.

On the way back to Vera's biology class, a flash of light zooms past me and into Ms. Kitchin's room. It can only be Warren. I rush to the English classroom in time to see the ball of light morph into a familiar Guardian standing inside Ms. Kitchin's classroom.

"Warren?"

He turns and looks at me.

"Nanette. Sorry, I must have missed you there."

"You missed Vera's entire English class. Have you been gone all day?"

Warren runs his hands through his wavy hair. "I've been doing some research."

"On what?"

"Hard to explain. Just trying to figure out what's made Ms. Kitchin feel like life's not worth living anymore."

"Did you find anything?" I peek past him into the classroom. Ms. Kitchin has a period of upperclassmen working in groups.

Warren looks over his shoulder at them. "Maybe."

"Like what?"

Warren turns back to me but ignores my question. "Where's Vera?"

"Biology."

"You should be with her."

"You left Ms. Kitchin alone for hours."

"I had my reasons." His answer is curt.

"Fine." I back up into the hallway. "I'll see you tomorrow ...maybe."

Warren doesn't respond. He simply glides to his Charge.

I sigh and return to mine.

At the end of the day, Vera heads back to her locker. She takes one glance at the literary magazine's flyer, pulls it right off and slaps it on another locker a few feet to her right.

I'm furious. She has no idea how hard I had to concentrate to carry that flyer down here and stick it on her locker. I have half a mind to yank it down right in front of her. As Vera begins to twirl the dial on her lock, I decide, *Why not?* She'll probably think the tape wore off. I glide over to the flyer, think about that crazy skit we did in drama club about the presidential election, and tug down on the flyer. It floats beautifully down to the speckled linoleum floor.

Vera ignores it. I want to kick it right to her, but I'm distracted by Cecille, who's pulled up to her own locker. I examine her face for signs of more crying. Her eyes don't look puffy or red, and I don't see any shadows nearby, so I hope whatever upset her yesterday was temporary.

Vera is almost all packed up when a familiar face passes

by. Gregory Hicks from the drama club is now standing next to my sister. With that scraggly little beard, he looks so much older than when I knew him as a gangly freshman. His body's filled out more now — his shoulders broader, his muscles more defined.

"Hey, little Dunston," he says. *Little Dunston?* He's calling her by her last name, by *our* last name. I guess that makes me *Big Dunston.* It hits me that I haven't been entirely forgotten.

Cecille looks up at him from under her pale lashes. "Hey." Her eyes return to her locker.

"You coming to drama club after school?"

Cecille nods without looking at him.

"Good. Cardone wants you to pick out a piece for the oral interp comp. Says he's got some good poems and monologues for you if you don't have your own."

"Right. Sure. I'll be there in a few minutes." Her head is practically buried in her locker as she rearranges her books.

Gregory slaps my sister on the shoulder. "Great. See ya then." He backs up right into Vera as she slams her locker shut. "Whoa, sorry there. Didn't see ya." Gregory moves on down the hall.

"Nobody ever does," Vera mutters. She looks like she wants to sink right into herself and disappear.

My sister pulls her head out of her locker and turns to look at Vera.

"Say something to her," I beg. "Make friends with her, Cecille. She needs one. You probably could use more, too."

Vera continues down the hall, and my sister kneels down to mess with the books at the bottom of her locker, but after a moment, she just stares at them for a bit. I kneel down next to her, fully aware that I should be following Vera.

"Cecille," I say the words out loud even though I know she can't hear me. "What's wrong, baby sister? I know what

111

I let you see was so, so wrong, but that was two years ago now and you were always the strong one. What's made you so sad?"

She's so still I have the crazy idea that maybe she can hear me. Then she reaches for one last book, tosses it into her bag, and stands up. I follow her as far as the theater door. When she opens it, I see the drama geeks inside. My heart aches. I want to be there with them. I want to memorize lines again. I want opening night jitters. I want the give and take of a good onstage dialogue when the chemistry between you and the other actor clicks and you're transported to this other world where you get to be somebody else for a while.

The auditorium door closes behind Cecille, but I can still hear the buzzing chatter of the kids. Their energy is infectious. And yet heartbreaking for me at the same time.

The moment I hear Mr. Cardone's voice telling them it's time to start the meeting, I bolt. I can't take anymore. It's too much for me to hear what I've left behind by taking my own life.

A memory rushes forth. I'm on the stage, wearing a white dress, and my hair's tied back in a little blue ribbon. A graveyard of dead people sits in chairs stage right. Stage left has the barest essentials of a kitchen.

It's my junior year, and I'm playing Emily Webb in *Our Town*. We're nearing the end, and I'm worked up to a fever pitch. My character has died, but has asked the stage manager if she can return to relive just one small moment in her life. The memory of her birthday proves too much for her to handle. I turn to the senior girl playing my mama. The words run through my head like it was yesterday.

"Oh, Mama," I say, "look at me one minute as though you really saw me. Mama, fourteen years have gone by. I'm dead. You're a grandmother, Mama! Wally's dead, too. His appendix burst on a camping trip to North Conway. We felt just terrible about it - don't you remember? But, just for a moment now we're all together. Mama, just for a moment we're happy. Let's really look at one another!"

As Emily Webb, I take in my surroundings at the old Webb home. "I can't. I can't go on. It goes so fast. We don't have time to look at one another. I didn't realize. So all that was going on and we never noticed. Take me back -- up the hill -- to my grave. But first: Wait! One more look. Good-bye, Good-bye world. Good-bye, Grover's Corners...Mama and Papa. Good-bye to clocks ticking...and Mama's sunflowers. And food and coffee. And new ironed dresses and hot baths...and sleeping and waking up. Oh, earth, you are too wonderful for anybody to realize you."

I turn to the stage manager. Usually the part is played by a man, but Mr. Cardone has cast a girl. "Do any human beings ever realize life while they live it—every, every minute?"

"No," she says. "The saints and poets, maybe—they do some."

The stage manager's words echo in my soul: "the saints and poets, maybe—they do some." I'm not a saint, and I'm not a poet, and I never realized what I was throwing away.

I'm at Vera's house before I know it. She turns the key in her front door, and a shadow follows her.

"No!" I scream as I chase after them. I shove myself between Vera and the shadow. "No! You don't get to have her. You don't get to have any of them!"

Vera tosses her bag down on a couch and heads for the kitchen.

"Stay away from her," my voice is venomous. The shadow floats in front of me. "I'm Guarding her. She's mine, not yours."

Above the howl of the shadow's stormy winds, I barely

hear Vera's phone buzz. She heads back to the living room to pull the phone out of her bag. I stay in the kitchen. Two knives gleam on the magnetic strip above the sink. "Saints and poets," I mutter to myself as I pull the knives off the strip and shove them into the open dishwasher with other dirty dishes. I'm contemplating emptying any knives from the silverware drawer when Vera walks back in, the shadow right behind her. The face has formed by now. It's Tamesis again.

Vera hits a few keys and then shoves her phone in her pocket. She looks at the magnetic knife strip and frowns. She opens the fridge, stares at the contents, and then closes the door with a sigh.

Vera stops at a calendar tacked onto the wall. She flips from October to November and points to Friday, the second. It's the same day I saw circled on a calendar last night.

"Soon," she mutters before sliding her finger off the calendar and letting the page fall back to October. She trudges upstairs. Tamesis and I follow.

Vera heads into her dad's room. Opening a drawer, she pulls out a tiny razor blade.

"Vera." My voice is barely audible even to me. "No, Vera. Not the cutting again." I put myself right in front of her.

Tamesis's inky darkness spreads out and fills the room. "She is mine," moans the shadow.

"Leave her!" I scream. Tamesis only grows larger. Her head towers a foot above me, and a dark pair of wings spread out the width of the small bedroom. The look of pleasure on her grotesque face is nauseating.

I turn back to Vera. "Don't do this, Vera. We'll find a reason for you to live. I didn't see the beauty in the world until it was too late, but you still can." The darkness spreads and gets thicker, like a fog rolling in. "There's beauty in the simple things, Vera. What about your poetry? Think of your poetry. Think about what Ms. Kitchin wrote on your paper today." Vera holds up the razor blade. I can barely see her through the darkness now. "Vera. Stop!"

Darkness falls, and I see nothing.

Chapter Sixteen

I see nothing that entire night. No huddled shape crying. No drops of blood on blue bathroom tile. Nothing.

When light finally returns, Vera's in the kitchen, emptying a box of chocolate krispies into a cereal bowl. The morning sun slants its dull autumn rays through the window over the sink.

Vera's dad walks in, his construction hat tucked under his arm. "I'll be late again tonight. Don't wait up." He grabs a protein shake from the fridge.

"We're out of cereal." Vera's head droops over her bowl. Her spoon pushes the chocolate krispies through a sea of milk.

Her dad pulls his wallet from his back pocket and removes a twenty. He tosses the bill on the kitchen table before walking out.

Almost immediately the wind howls, and I'm back in the dark before I can even see the shadows approaching.

The time I spend in the dark seems to stretch like a rubber band. Sometimes the moments go by quickly, and I'm in the light again before I know it. Other times I wonder if the darkness will ever end.

When I'm aware of the seconds passing, as I am now, I wonder what is happening to Vera. Is she cutting herself again? Will this time be the last? Which cut will be the one that severs the artery and lets all the life spill out of her?

With so much time to think, I doubt my ability to help her at all. How can I save her when I couldn't save myself? What if my wings never grow in—does that mean I can't save her? I must help Vera see that she has something to contribute to this world, and so far the only positive thing I've found is the comment from Ms. Kitchin.

First period is P.E. I sneak out of the gym during free throw drills to tack the neon-green literary magazine flyer back onto Vera's locker. She doesn't see it until after Introduction to Art (period 2) when she yanks it off with a sigh and stabs it onto the locker next to hers.

During period 3 English, I slip out during a short story reading and move the neon green flyer back to Vera's locker. I am nothing if not determined. Besides, Warren has ditched English class for the second day in a row. If I'm not getting any new training, I might as well use flyer moving as practice.

After Ms. Kitchin's class, Vera heads to her locker again. She fumes with anger when she sees the flyer again. The boy with the locker next to hers throws down his books and twists his lock.

"Are you the one doing this?" Vera shoves the paper in the boy's face.

He's a short, dorky kid with glasses, and I've never heard him say a word to anyone.

"What?" He looks as surprised that Vera's speaking to him as I'm surprised by the ferocity of her anger. Her expression is usually either gloomy or passive. I've never seen this much emotion from her.

"This!" She waves the flyer. "It keeps ending up on my locker."

The boy shrugs. "It's not me." He shuffles books around.

Vera frowns, crumbles the paper, and grabs her geometry book. The flyer gets tossed in a garbage can on the way to Mr. Gallagher's class.

Poor Vera has no idea how stubborn I can be. During the geometry test, I roam the halls to find another neon green flyer. I have to be careful to pick one in a vacant hallway where no one will see me moving it. I almost giggle at the idea of someone seeing the neon flyer floating through the hallway like it's moving of its own accord.

The urge to giggle stops when I notice my own picture hanging in a display case. I float closer. I had forgotten our school had this case. Inside is an "In Memoriam" section dedicated to kids who passed away while students here. I never paid much attention to it while I was in high school. It seemed a little creepy to see the photos of kids who died. But now there's one of me added to the group. They used my senior class picture, of course. Not a bad photo of me. I put my angel hand against the glass. I could push right through the glass to touch my picture, but I don't. I just stand and marvel at how pretty my hair had looked that day.

Afraid the tears will come again, I start to turn away but stop when I notice another picture. Tammy Ringles. The older sister of Cathy Ringles, the dance team girl I'd seen holding center court in the cafeteria. The newspaper article about Tammy's tragic car accident is pinned next to her photo. Like me, she'd been a senior when she died. Funny how two younger sisters could react so differently to having an older sister die. Tammy's sister Cathy throws her nose up in the air and becomes the center of attention. Cecille puts her head down and ends up chased by shadows.

Back at Vera's locker, I decide not to tape it on the front. Instead, I fold the paper and shove it through the vents in the locker. The folding takes a lot of concentrating. Several times I stop and think about something good from my life. I remember how Ally and I once laughed so hard during a romantic movie we were asked to leave the theater. We couldn't help it if the lead actor reminded us of our science teacher and we got the giggles thinking of him making the moves on the lead actress, who looked like our favorite waitress from the local diner.

By the time I get the flyer folded small enough to fit into

the vent, I cry about Ally's death all over again. How could God have taken her from me? Even death hadn't brought me Ally again. I'm sure Ally must be in heaven. She probably went straight to sainthood after the car accident. No angelhood business for her.

I'm ready to give up on Vera, but the thought of making it to sainthood and seeing Ally again — and knowing that when I do, she'll make me laugh — gives me the strength to push the flyer through the locker vent.

When Vera stops at her locker before lunch, the neon flyer falls to the speckled linoleum floor. Vera looks around the hallway like she expects someone to be watching her to see how she'll react. Of course, none of the other kids are looking because none of them are involved. Poor Vera has no idea she's being haunted by her own Guardian.

A few shouts down the hallway make me turn my head. A young boy shoves another kid. Before the second boy can shove him back, Ms. Kitchin steps out of her classroom. Vera looks at Ms. Kitchin, then at the flyer in her hand. Quickly, she takes what she needs out of her locker, slams it, and walks toward Ms. Kitchin.

Having swiftly ended the scuffle, Ms. Kitchin shoos away the onlookers. Vera walks right through the small crowd.

"Ms. Kitchin, did you put this in my locker?"

The English teacher reaches for the flyer and unfolds it. "Oh, the literary magazine. No, I didn't put this in your locker, but it's a good idea for you."

"Someone keeps putting a copy of it on my locker."

Ms. Kitchin smiles. "It sounds like someone else has discovered your talent."

Vera shakes her head. "No one's read my poems but you."

"You must have shown them to someone else. Friends?

Family?"

Vera shakes her head again.

"That's too bad. I think some of your classmates could relate to your poem 'Colors'." Ms. Kitchin refolds the flyer and hands it back to Vera. "You really should submit it."

"I don't think that'd be such a great idea," Vera says.

"Well, I suppose you could be like Emily Dickinson. Write a ton of poems, tie them up in bundles, and let others discover them when you're dead."

Vera's eyes widen. I fear Ms. Kitchin is giving her ideas.

"But what fun would that be, Vera? We write to share our thoughts with the world, to know that we've touched another heart. Don't miss this opportunity to share your words with others."

The bell rings and Ms. Kitchin returns to her classroom.

Clutching the flyer, Vera heads off to lunch.

"She's right, Vera." I glide alongside her and talk out loud even though she can't hear me. "It's the same reason I enjoyed acting in plays. I always got audience feedback. From their laughter, I knew if I was being funny. If I was doing a serious scene and the theater was dead silent, I knew I had their hearts in a dramatic lurch. And when they applauded at the end, I knew I'd made some difference in their lives, even if it was just a small one. If I'd acted in an empty theater, it wouldn't have been the same. Not submitting your writing is like trying to act in an empty room. What's the point?"

Oh God, I wish she could hear me.

At lunch, Vera looks back and forth between the flyer and her poem. After eating her ham and cheese sandwich and refolding her aluminum foil into a perfect square, she takes out a pencil and begins to revise the poem. I peek over her shoulder. The poem reads:

One morning when I woke up,

I felt something was lacking.
The color yellow had left.
It simply had gone missing.

It wasn't in the sun
When it rose above shore.
It wasn't in the daffodils
Right outside my door.

By lunchtime, green was also gone.
Who knows where it had fled?
The trees around me all went brown.
The grass looked simply dead.

Purple faded in the afternoon.
The lilacs all looked dull.
At dinner, the color red was next
To take its curtain call.

By sunset, pink and orange
Had said their last adieu.
It used to be so pretty.
Now the sky is barely blue.

When morning came,
I hoped for change.
But blue was last to go
And only gray remained.

I'm tired of feeling numb.
I want to see the light.
I'm sick of looking at a world
That's only black and white.

Where did all the colors go?

I don't bother putting any more flyers on Vera's locker. If she doesn't take the hint now, there's nothing else I can do. The deadline for submissions is tonight.

At home, I stay with Vera instead of falling into the darkness. She heads to the computer in the den and goes to the school's website. Quickly, she types her revised poem into an email addressed to the magazine. Then she hesitates, her cursor hovering over the send button.

"C'mon, Vera." I bend down, hovering over her right shoulder. "You can do this. Ms. Kitchin would want you to do this."

Vera pulls her hand off the mouse and bites her right forefinger knuckle.

"Don't be nervous, Vera. Just hit the button. What's the worst they can do? Reject you? So what? Everyone gets rejected. If they don't like the poem, find someone else who does, or write another poem."

I straighten up. *What am I saying? Everyone gets rejected?* It's true, but why hadn't I thought of that before? When DePaul's Theater School had rejected me, why hadn't I thought of other ways to get into acting? I mean, I did ...kind of. But the truth was that I lost faith. I didn't think I could do it any other way. I assumed if one theater school thought I wasn't good enough, that everyone else would feel the same. I hadn't even given myself a chance.

"C'mon, Vera. Be braver than I was." The original poem with Ms. Kitchin's comments and Vera's revisions scribbled in pencil sits on the edge of the desk. I blow in the direction of the paper. The page bends slightly, enough to catch Vera's eye. She picks up the page. Her eyes scan Ms. Kitchin's words. She curls her lower lip up under her teeth and hits the send button.

"Nice job, Vera. Now we just sit and wait."

And pray.

Chapter Seventeen

For the next few days, the shadows stay away. Unfortunately, so does Warren. I worry my training will never be complete.

Then, out of the blue, Warren shows up in Vera's art class. He pokes his head right through the classroom wall and looks around until he spots me.

"Nanette! Great, I found you." Warren passes the rest of the way through the wall.

"Where have you been? You're supposed to be training me, and I haven't seen you in nearly a week."

"Yeah, sorry about that. Listen, I need a favor."

"What?"

"I need to be away again today."

I open my mouth to protest, but Warren doesn't give me a chance.

"I need you to keep an eye on Ms. Kitchin for me while you're in English class with Vera. If she starts talking about babies or birthdays, create some sort of diversion—knock over a stack of books or clang some lockers out in the hallway—anything that will change the subject."

"Warren, what on Earth are you talking about?"

"I'm onto something, Nanette. I'm really close to solving this one. I've just got to confirm one more suspicion I have, and then I'll know how to help her get through this."

"What suspicion?"

"I don't have time to explain. I've got to check something out, and the best time for me to be away is while you're in the room with her. I don't want to leave her alone any more than possible." His gaze turns inward. "Especially not at this time of year."

The bell rings and the students all gather their books.

"You're headed to English now, right?" he says.

"Yeah."

"Good. I'll be back as fast as can." Warren pulls away.

"Wait!" I follow him out to the hall.

"Just keep her off of babies and birthdays!" Warren spreads his shimmering wings, and before I can say any more, he's a speeding ball of light hurtling through the crowded hall.

I float behind Vera on the way to English. What on Earth could Warren have figured out? *Babies and birthdays?*

During class, I examine Ms. Kitchin. She looks to be in her late thirties. Maybe she wanted to be a mother but never got the chance. Maybe her birthday's coming up, and she doesn't want to be reminded that she's so old. If that's the case, what is Warren researching?

Luckily, neither babies nor birthdays come up as topics as the class begins reading *Romeo and Juliet*. I am, however, fearful of how the ending of this play will impact Vera. I'm hoping the not-so-happy ending doesn't give Vera any ideas.

Warren is in English class the next day. He's sitting in the back of the room, just like I found him the first day we met. However, this time he doesn't look like a misplaced upperclassman in a freshman English class. Instead, he slumps in his chair like a guy who's fought one too many battles.

"You're back," I say when Vera and I enter the room. I want to ask him a million questions right away, but his sad eyes make me hold back.

"Yup." Warren nods.

"What happened?"

"I found what I was looking for."

"That's great. Now you can help Ms. Kitchin."

Warren simply shakes his head.

"Why not?"

Warren sighs before saying, "Remember how I told you I'd been abandoned as a baby at a church?" He doesn't look at me as he talks. He stares at the front of the room while attendance is taken.

"Yeah."

"I was shuffled from foster home to foster home. As I got older, I asked the usual questions about where I'd come from, who my parents were, why I'd been abandoned."

I nod encouragement so Warren will keep talking.

"Yesterday I found out how I came to be abandoned at a church."

"What do you mean?"

"My mother was too young to care for me. She was unwed and scared."

"I don't understand. I thought you went to follow up on a hunch you had about Ms. Kitchin."

"I did." His eyes are still focused on the front of the room. It's starting to creep me out the way he won't look at me.

"Then how did you find out about your mother?"

Warren finally changes his gaze so that he's looking at me. Perhaps it's the sadness in his eyes that finally makes the pieces click for me.

"Ms. Kitchin," I whisper her name and look at the front of the room. "She's your mother."

"She was only seventeen at the time. Her parents had kicked her out of the house."

"Oh boy." I sit down at the desk next to Warren. "Is this why she...why she..."

"Why the shadows are haunting her? Yeah, I think so. I think she really regrets what she did. She thought she'd have plenty of time to have children later, but it never happened for her."

"How did you figure it out?"

Warren sits up a little in his seat. "I've been guarding her for a little over a year. Last year she took off of work on my birthday. At first I thought it was just a coincidence, but this year she visited the church where she left me. Started asking if anyone there had been around twenty-one years ago when a baby was left in the back pew."

"What are you going to do now?"

"I don't know." His gaze shifts to Ms. Kitchin.

I look at her and marvel at the fact that she has no idea her son's spirit has been guarding her for over a year.

"I thought you and Matthew and Betsy said the Committee doesn't place Guardians in situations that are too close to home. You thought my being placed at my old high school was a mistake. They placed you with your own mother!"

"I went to see Joshua at the basilica last night. He wouldn't tell me why they'd placed me with my mom—only that it hadn't been a mistake." Warren scratches his head like he's trying to rub away the thoughts plaguing his mind. "She's trying to find me."

"What?"

"She doesn't know I killed myself. She's trying to figure out what happened to the baby boy she left at the church. She wants to know that he grew up healthy and strong and happy."

I look at Warren's angelic soul seated next to me. "Oh God."

"Exactly. If she finds out I took my own life, she'll never heal. The shadows will come, and I don't know if I can stop them."

We sit for a few minutes, looking at Ms. Kitchin. I try to imagine a way to help her. As she walks amid the students, I see in her eyes a deep sadness. I've always seen something of it before, but now, knowing what's behind that sadness, makes me realize how deep it runs in her.

Days pass. Sometimes Warren is in English class and sometimes he's not. When he leaves, it's because he's trying to find ways to cover up his suicide so that Ms. Kitchin will never know her baby boy didn't think his own life was worth living. Leaving during Vera's English class is the best time for him to go since I can cover for him, but it's awful for me because it means I get less training.

At first I argue with him to stay because I need my training and if I'm stronger I may be able to help him. I give that up after a while. On the days when he doesn't run off, he's so morose that my training barely progresses. Out in the hallway I practice bending paper clips, opening locks, and tying and untying smelly gym shoes the kids have in their lockers.

Warren tells me my wings are growing, but they're not big enough for me to unfurl yet. Once again, I lament the fact that angels have no reflections. If only I could look in a mirror, I could turn around and see the progress my wings are making.

At night, I follow Vera home. Sometimes I'm able to stay with her through the night, but sometimes the shadows are waiting, and they're too powerful for me to stop. Her dad is rarely home. Vera spends a lot of time typing on her computer or writing in her thorny heart notebook.

On Saturday she spends hours looking through photos on her computer. Most of them are of her and her parents. She spends a really long time on any picture that includes her mom.

Later in the afternoon, she heads to the cemetery down the street from her church. It doesn't take me long to guess why we're there. Flat against the earth is a simple headstone for Ann Lavoy, Vera's mother. I'm not surprised Vera visits there, but the date on the tombstone makes me quiver. Mrs. Lavoy had passed away on November 2, two years ago. November 2 is the date I keep seeing circled on calendars.

Belphagor said Vera had already picked out the day of her death. Is she planning on ending her life on the anniversary of her mother's death? If that's true, I have only a couple weeks left to change her mind.

On the day the literary magazine comes out, copies are distributed in homeroom. Vera flips through the pages rapidly. She stops suddenly on page 10. There she finds her poem "Colors," accompanied by a student's drawing of the world losing all its color.

A rare smile on Vera's face tells me all I need to know. At that moment, an itching in my back makes me want to reach up and scratch, but my right hand passes over something soft when I put it behind me. Over my shoulder, I see the top curve of a luminescent wing. I turn to the left to its twin on the other side. With an effort, I am able to spread them out. They're not as wide as Warren's, but they stretch out almost as far as my fingertips. I concentrate some more in order to move them, but I'm about as steady with them as a toddler taking its first steps. Probably not a good idea to attempt flying right away.

I hope Warren is feeling up to giving me flying lessons. Maybe we can meet tonight on the rooftop. The garden up there would be the perfect place to take my first few gliding leaps.

Vera tucks the magazine under her books and carries it with her all day. I'm so excited to see Warren and show him my wings, but he heads out of Ms. Kitchin's room as soon as Vera and I enter.

"Good. You're here," he says as I walk in. "Watch her.

I'll be gone all period."

"Warren, wait!" I grab his arm as he heads out. "Look." I turn for him and wave my wings. "I can unfurl them!"

By the absent-minded nod of his head, I'm not sure he sees me at all. "Awesome." He turns to go.

"Wait! Aren't you going to teach me to fly?"

He hesitates. "Sure. When I get the chance." He spreads his wings out in the hallway. The bell has rung, and the final stragglers enter class.

"How about tonight? We could meet on the rooftop."

"Sure." He pumps his wings once.

Before I can say more, he's a ball of shimmering light flying through the hallway. With a sigh, I return to Ms. Kitchin's room. She looks the saddest I've seen her yet. I hope Warren can solve the problem soon. Of course, if he does, that means he'll be going the way of Betsy, and then who do I turn to for help? Matthew? Certainly, I can't turn to the newest Guardian at school. Although there have been glimmers of Elizabeth Wolf coming into shape, she's still spending most of her time as pure light. If Warren moves on to sainthood, I don't know what I'll do.

Chapter Eighteen

After English, Vera heads back to her locker. I almost stop following her when I see Cecille at hers. In her hands is an open copy of the literary magazine.

She's reading Vera's poem.

As usual, Vera has her head down and does not realize my sister is reading her words. She heads straight to her locker and begins maneuvering books.

"Did you write this?" Cecille practically shoves the magazine, folded open to Vera's poem, under her nose.

"Yes." Vera's voice is small, almost as if she hopes that by saying it quietly she's somehow not admitting it.

"It's really good." Cecille takes the magazine back.

Vera continues switching out books. My sister bites her lip.

"I know what you mean. About the colors disappearing. That's the way I've been feeling lately."

If I still had lungs, I would be holding my breath. Is it possible my sister's about to spill what's been plaguing her? I haven't seen any shadows whirling through the school toward her, but that doesn't mean she hasn't been plagued outside of school.

Vera glances shyly at Cecille. "Something bad happen?"

"Yeah."

I hang there waiting for more. Vera looks like she's waiting too, but then she slams her locker shut.

"My Aunt Tippy died from breast cancer last year." My sister blurts it out so suddenly that both Vera and I stop in our tracks. What have I missed since my death? Aunt Tippy's dead? She didn't have breast cancer when I died.

"I'm sorry," Vera whispers.

"Now my mom's got it, and I'm worried she's going to

die too. The doctors said it's stage four. They're doing some really aggressive chemo." My sister wipes at a tear that has wiggled its way out despite her attempts to keep control. "I want someone to tell me everything's going to be okay."

Vera shifts the books in her hands. "I've got to get to class." She bolts down the hall, and I know I should follow, but I can't leave my sister.

Mom has cancer?

Cecille rubs her eyes and then closes her own locker. Only a few students remain in the hall. Never before have I missed the ability to talk so much. There are so many things I want to say to my baby sister. I want to be the one to tell her that Mom's going to be okay. I want to put my arm around her and tell her not to worry. Mom's a strong woman. She'll make it through.

Why wasn't I there to help her through all this? My own selfish act took me away, and now my poor sister has to deal with this alone. Dad is probably no help; besides, he lives in another house now. Who's there when Mom gets sick from her treatments? Who keeps the house clean? Who makes the meals?

A wind howls, and a storm cloud heads our way. I use my wing tip to jiggle a lock behind me. It's enough to wake Cecille to the fact that the hall is almost empty.

"C'mon, Cecille, keep moving. Let's get to class."

Cecille glances at a digital clock suspended from the ceiling, then hurries down the hall. I follow her and stay with her through her next class. The shadow hovers outside the door the entire time. It swirls there, not really forming a shape or a face, so I can't tell if it's Tamesis or not. Whenever it looks like it's about to enter, I move something in the room—a pencil, a paper, a book—anything to distract Cecille from the evil thoughts I know are plaguing her mind.

I don't feel comfortable leaving Cecille until lunch. She

sits with her theater friends and they are enough to keep her content.

Instead of going to Vera, I head off to see if Warren has returned, but he's not in Ms. Kitchin's room. I even go to the athletic department to find Matthew.

"Sorry, Nanette." As he talks, Matthew follows around a middle-aged man wearing a black t-shirt with "Coach" written on the back. "I haven't seen Warren in ages. We used to meet up once a week to discuss our Charges, but he hasn't shown lately. He's knee deep in something."

Either Warren hasn't told Matthew yet that his Charge is his own mother or Matthew doesn't think I should know.

I thank Matthew anyway and head off to find Vera. She's holding it together in German class. I'm thankful Frau Meinz has decided today's a good day for practicing German folk songs. From my limited time as a Guardian, I've learned that happy music seems to keep all sorts of demons away.

For the rest of the school day, I fly between Vera's classes and Cecille's. I don't know her schedule, so it takes a while to figure out where she is each period. Once I find her, I stick with her until that period's over and follow her to the next. Then I check on Vera.

At the end of the day, Cecille gets into Mom's car in the parking lot. The scarf around Mom's head makes sense now. Part of me wants to hop right in the car with them, throw my arms around Mom, and never let go. Another part of me knows that if I do that, if I see my mom close up—without eyebrows and eyelashes—I won't be able to handle it, and Belphagor might as well come for me.

Praying that my sister can stay strong while she's with Mom, I chase after Vera. She's home just before me, and the darkness swallows me before I can follow her up to her room.

I don't know why the shadows have such a hold over

Vera's house. Is it because I don't get there until after she does? Or is there something going on in the house that brings Vera into such a state of depression?

The light doesn't return until morning. I groan when I realize I missed my flying lesson with Warren. What is he going to think? He'll probably be mad. I couldn't help it if the shadows knocked me senseless before I could put up a fight. I'll simply have to apologize. That's assuming he even shows up at school today.

Despite my best attempts at prayer, there is no sign of Warren when Vera and I enter English class. In fact, there's no sign of Ms. Kitchin either. There's a lot of talk going on while the substitute is trying to take attendance, but I don't notice at first. My thoughts are on Warren and Ms. Kitchin. Where could they both be right now?

"Hey," an obnoxiously loud boy from the back row calls out as soon as the sub finishes attendance. "Where's Ms. Kitchin? That woman's never sick."

The sub shrugs. "I don't know. I got a call at 6:30 this morning saying there was an emergency, and I needed to come in."

"Is Ms. Kitchin all right?" the boy next to Vera asks.

"I'm sure she'll be fine."

"*Be* fine? That sounds like she's not fine now."

The sub hesitates. He looks like he'd like to swallow his last few words. "I didn't mean to imply that anything was wrong with her. I only know that I got called in last minute."

Next to me, Vera takes out the literary magazine. She looks again at her poem, then shuts the magazine with a sigh.

By eighth period, I'm exhausted from running back and forth between Vera's and Cecille's classes. I can't possibly keep this up. I rush to find the only nearby Guardian who might be able to help.

"Matthew, have you heard anything from Warren?"

He shakes his head. Behind him the assistant football coach is running basketball drills in eighth period P.E.

"Ms. Kitchin's not here."

"So he's probably with her."

"The sub made it sound like something happened to her. Matthew, what would happen to Warren if Ms. Kitchin...you know?"

"If Ms. Kitchin became a lifer, like you and Warren?"

I nod, unable to say the words.

"I don't know, to be honest. I mean, if Warren's supposed to be keeping her from suicide and she goes ahead and does it anyway, then I'm thinking he's in pretty big trouble."

"But he can't control her. It's not his fault if she gives up! What about free will and all that?"

Matthew follows the coach as he walks down the sidelines.

"Maybe he gets a second chance. Maybe he's assigned a new Charge."

"Have you heard of that happening before?"

"All I've ever heard of are Guardians moving on to sainthood or Guardians giving up and turning themselves over to Belphagor."

The idea of Warren being wrapped in Belphagor's dozen tongues of flame while he burns to a crisp is more than I can bear.

"Matthew, I need help. I can't watch Vera and Cecille at the same time."

"Whoa, wait. Isn't Cecille your sister? You're trying to watch your Charge and your sister at the same time?"

"I have to. I can't let my sister fall to the shadows. Matthew, I need more skills, I need more grace. I need something big, like Joshua's ability to take a human form."

"Only the best of the best can do that, Nanette."

"Then what else am I supposed to do? Moving around little objects isn't enough to make either my sister or Vera feel like life is worth living."

"It takes time."

"I don't have time. Cecille's losing it because our mom has cancer. If Mom dies, there's no way I can be there for Cecille *and* Vera. I can't even see Vera at night. She falls to the shadows almost every day after school. I'm left in total darkness most nights. When I see her again in the morning, she's got a new cut somewhere on her body. If I don't do something soon, this girl's going to cut too much and bleed out on me."

The coach blows his whistle. "Enough for today. Go get changed."

"Nanette, I've got to take care of him. Coach is always at his worst between classes. Listen, I have only one idea for you."

"What? I'll do anything."

"You need to head back to Our Lady of Sorrows."

"The church?"

He nods. "The basilica where the Committee meets."

"Why?"

"In the back of the church is a small chapel dedicated to Mary. There's a replica of Michelangelo's *Pietà* in there. You know what that is?"

"It's a statue, right?"

"Yeah, Mary's holding Jesus in her arms right after he's taken off the cross. In that chapel, sometimes, if you're lucky, you'll get to talk with Sophy."

"Who's Sophy?"

"She was a Guardian back in the 1920s. When she was alive, she had a little too much fun at the speakeasies, got into a car, and crashed it. For her angelhood, she was assigned another flapper with a drinking problem. She had so much fun helping her Charge see the light that when she made it to heaven—in record-breaking time, I hear—she asked God if she could return and guard more souls. She got so good at it that she no longer acts as a Guardian herself. Instead, she's become something of a mentor to other Guardians. The problem is that she's in high demand. Everyone wants advice from Sophy."

"So what do I do? Just head to the basilica and wait in line?"

"No, she's not always at Our Lady of Sorrows. When I said everyone wants advice from Sophy, I mean *everyone*. She spends all her time running from church to church. She only goes where the prayers and the needs are the greatest. If you want to speak with her, you'll have to get into the chapel and pray your little heart out."

My hopes sink. I've never been good at prayer. "Could you go and ask her for me?"

Matthew laughs. "No, Sophy would never go for that. The desire has to come from you."

The kids are all out of the gym by now and on their way to the locker rooms. Coach picks up the last of the basketballs.

"I gotta go, Nanette."

I need to get back to Vera and Cecille, too, but one last question has to be asked. "Matthew, can you teach me how to fly? Warren was going to do it, but now he's disappeared."

Matthew smiles as he follows the Coach out of the gym. "You've got your wings, Nanette. All you need now is a little faith. You'll find that many things in angelhood, as in life, are simply a matter of having the right tools and believing in the power of God."

Chapter Nineteen

If I were still alive, what I'm about to do would be downright suicidal. The irony of it all hits me as I stand on the precipice of the school's rooftop garden.

After school today, I did my best to get to Vera's house before she did. I laid out some of her favorite stuffed animals on her pink comforter. When she got home and saw them, she smiled. I had noticed them laid out this way in some of the photos from when she was a kid. I'd hoped she'd think her dad had done it for her.

Then I knocked her iPod off the dresser so she'd think of listening to some music. Anything I could think of to lighten her mood and keep the shadows away was used. When she was fast asleep, I ran over to school.

As I look out over the soccer fields and the baseball diamonds, I replay Matthew's words: "You'll find that many things in angelhood, as in life, are simply a matter of having the right tools and believing in the power of God."

"Okay, God. I need to get to the basilica. I've got the tools. I have the wings. I even googled directions to the basilica on Vera's computer when she was in the bathroom. So give me the power, God. I've got to talk with Sophy."

I look down over the parapet's edge. It's a three-story drop to the concrete sidewalk below. It's a good thing I'm already dead because this drop could kill me. I take a deep breath and spread my wings, a skill I practiced all evening while watching Vera. The wings stretch out beyond my fingertips now.

"Be with me, God." My knees bend and I drop off the edge.

My eyes are closed, but I can feel myself falling. Then suddenly I feel a contraction in my back and I'm no longer plummeting toward the Earth. The wings beat gently behind me, and I'm soaring over the treetops. The sight of streetlamps and random cars passing below me is even more beautiful than the night Warren had flown me to the meeting.

I enjoy the flying so much I almost forget to look where I am going, but when I recognize a certain stretch of highway below, I realize I'm getting close and veer to the west.

My landing is a little rough. I need to take several extra steps to stop my momentum, but I land successfully on the street in front of Our Lady of Sorrows. The street is dark and quiet except for a few passing cars. After tucking my wings behind me, I walk up the steps and through the first set of doors. I stop momentarily before the inner red doors embossed with the letters S and M. I never did get to ask Warren what they meant. Where is he tonight? Is he okay? Is Ms. Kitchin okay?

On the other side of the red doors, angels kneel in prayer. Not as many as the first night I was here but enough to remind me that I'm not the only one asking for God's help tonight. The basilica has about twelve little chapels that line the sides of the pews, six on each side. Matthew said to look for the one with the replica of the *Pietà* in it, but I don't see any statues that look like Mary holding a crucified Jesus. There's a dark highly stylized crucifix in one, and another chapel is dedicated to St. Therese, but I don't see what Matthew described.

Now what? Maybe Matthew was playing a joke on me. I wouldn't put it past the big jock.

"May I help you?"

Joshua stands behind me. He looks perfectly serene, as if nothing I could say would bother or offend him. I tilt my head to look up at him. Despite his towering size, his presence is calming, not intimidating.

"I'm looking for the chapel with the *Pietà* ...well, the

replica of it at least."

Joshua smiles. "Seeking Sophy's wisdom?"

I don't speak. I just nod.

Joshua lifts his right hand and gestures to a doorway located to the left of the altar.

I point and raise an eyebrow. The back of church seems like an odd place to be hiding an important statue, much less Sophy.

Joshua's smile widens and he walks away. I head toward the door. As I approach, another Guardian walks out. He is middle aged and haggard.

"Good luck," he says as he passes. "I've been praying for over an hour and no sign of her." Rather disgruntled, he marches away.

I walk through a hallway and enter a small dark chapel. The white marble statue stands on a raised platform. The walls behind it are dark red on top and white marble on the bottom. A small stained glass window depicts the baptism of Jesus in the Jordan. To my right is a dark wooden staircase that looks like it belongs in an old house, not the back of a church. I wonder where it could possibly lead. To my left, a red exit sign lights up the area near a set of double doors.

I step toward the *Pietà* and kneel on the lowest level of the platform right in front of it. The serenity on Mary's face captivates me. How could she be so calm when her son has been murdered? And yet Jesus himself looks peaceful too. I think about my own death. The moments right after it were anything but calm. There was chaos and confusion — darkness and light — but even the light only brought me more bewilderment. Why was I seeing scenes from a strange girl's life? Where was the peace I had sought when I decided to take my own life?

Maybe peace only comes when your death occurs as it should — and when it should — not when you've brought it on yourself.

I can't help it. I know I'm supposed to be praying for Sophy to appear, but instead I break down and cry. What was I thinking when I took my own life? Did I really think that would bring me peace and happiness? I'm suddenly overwhelmed by the moments in my life I'll never experience—another curtain call, laughing with friends, flirting with boys, marriage, children, college, being there for my sister as our mom battles cancer. Then there's all the simple things: a cup of hot cocoa after shoveling the snow on a winter afternoon, long walks in the fall while the leaves crunch under my feet, the summer sun warming my skin after a swim in Lake Michigan, rainbows that stretch across the sky after a spring rain.

Emily's speech at the end of *Our Town* makes more sense than ever before. I wish I could be like her and crawl back to my graveyard and not have to think about the lovely things I'll never know again. But I can't. Life isn't a Thornton Wilder play. I'm stuck here watching a girl who doesn't see the beauty in her own life. I watch her make dinner, and I think about how I'll never learn to cook. I watch her climb under her pink comforter, and I realize I'll never know the wonderful soft warmth of snuggling under the covers again. I watch her blush when the boy in English class smiles at her, and I know I'll never get a smile like that from a living boy again.

Oh, God, I was such an idiot!

"There, there now, darling. No need to get so worked up."

The soft voice from behind startles me. How long has someone been in the chapel with me? I stand up and wipe away my tears. I'm too ashamed to turn around and face the intruder right away.

"I'll be all right," I mutter.

"Of course, you will, dear. Everyone who asks for God's help receives it."

"I was actually hoping to meet Sophy." I turn to face the woman who has interrupted my self-pity session.

Behind me stands a twenty-something woman with a bobbed haircut and a felt hat pushed down low and tight on her head. She wears a pale blue dress with a drop waist and knee-length hem. Several layers of beads drip down the front. Her outfit reminds me of the flapper costume Ally wore for Halloween when we were in eighth grade.

"See? Ask and you shall receive," she says, opening her arms wide.

"Sophy?"

"Well, darling, what were you expecting? A grandmotherly sort?"

"But you died back in the 20s?"

"Yes, and I was 26 at the time." Sophy smiles. "Now let's get to business, shall we? I have many more Guardians to aid tonight."

"I need help…"

Sophy waves a hand and bangles jingle on her arm. "No need to go through all the details, dearie. I see and know much more than you can imagine. If you're going to help Vera, you'll have to get at what's really troubling her."

"I managed to get her poem published. She seemed happy about that."

"Her writing is a blessing to her. That's true. But what is it that really breaks her heart?"

"Her mother died of cancer."

Sophy clasps her hands behind her back and walks to stand before the *Pietà*. Staring at Mary holding Jesus, she says, "Death does cause much sorrow, but you can't bring back Vera's mom, just like you can't do anything to ease the pain your sister has felt since watching you die."

"Oh God." My tears rush forward again.

Sophy grabs hold of my shoulders. "Nanette, what else is breaking Vera's heart day after day after day?"

I stifle a sob. "She seems the worst when she goes home. I can't even see her sometimes; the shadows are too powerful. When I first started guarding her, she and her dad would eat dinner in silence. Now he's not even home for dinner at all — just texts her to say he's working late and not to wait for him. It's like her father is as dead to her as her own mother."

"Then you must do something about that."

"But how? All I can do is move small objects. If I could just talk to her. If I could be like Joshua and appear human to her, I could make a real difference."

"Nanette, that takes years of growing in grace." Sophy takes my hands. "But there is something you can do. You can whisper ideas to them."

I lift my tear-rimmed eyes to Sophy. "She could hear me?"

"Not exactly. It's more like planting little seeds of thought that can grow into wonderful ideas. Vera will think the idea just occurred to her out of the blue."

"Isn't that kind of like mind control?"

"No, humans always have a choice."

"So it's more like I'm the proverbial angel on the right shoulder while the shadows are the proverbial demon on the left shoulder. Vera still gets to decide which of us to listen to."

Sophy smiles. "Yes, I suppose that's a good comparison."

"So how do I do it?"

"With a little faith and God's help." Before I can question any more, Sophy lifts her hands and places them on my head. "Dear Lord, please grant Nanette the ability to believe that you will help her and in doing so, when her heart is pure and her intentions true, let her whisper your words into the hearts of your faithful. Amen."

143

My eyes are closed throughout the prayer. When I feel Sophy lift her hands off my head, I open my eyes and she's gone. The little chapel is empty.

Chapter Twenty

Was Sophy here, or had I imagined it? No, she had to have been here. I feel somehow...transformed. My wings are strong, and I fly back to the suburbs faster than before.

When I return to Vera's house, it's dark inside. Not just the darkness of night, but the darkness of the shadows. I don't even try to enter. I remain outside and spend the night praying for the right words to whisper to Vera when she awakes.

I hover by Vera's bedroom window, waiting for the alarm clock to go off, but when it does, the shadows are still too strong for me to enter. My plan for getting her to talk to her father during breakfast is thwarted. I can't whisper to her if I'll black out as soon as I enter the house.

Vera's dad leaves before she does. His pickup truck pulls out of the garage a half hour before Vera walks out the front door. Her eyes are puffy like she spent the night crying and huddled under that pink comforter.

She hesitates on the front step, one hand still on the doorknob.

"Don't even think about going back into that house, Vera. Put one foot in front of the other and get your butt to school."

She heaves a sigh and steps off the porch. I don't know if it's a coincidence or if I actually planted that suggestion in her head, but I'm glad she's moving.

At school, there's still no sign of Warren or Ms. Kitchin. Several times I stop by her classroom on my way between checking on Vera and Cecille. Although I'm disappointed, I feel it's really up to me now to save both my Charge and my sister. I don't care if the "rules" say the Charge has to want a Guardian. I'm not leaving my sister unprotected. In fact, I wonder if there's a way to help both of them at the same time.

The idea hits me when I'm watching Cecille and Vera at their lockers before fifth period. The tip of my wing knocks a magnetic pink ribbon off Vera's locker while I use my hands to pull the literary magazine off my sister's top locker shelf. Then I pray that Sophy was right about God giving me the ability to plant thoughts in people's minds as I lean over my sister and say, "Perform the poem."

My sister's eyes move from the pink ribbon on the floor to the magazine that has landed at her feet. She opens the magazine to Vera's poem.

"Vera." Cecille talks slowly like the idea is still forming in her head. "Would you mind if I used your poem as a performance piece for drama club?"

"What?" Vera shuts her locker and stares at my sister as if she's speaking a foreign language.

"For drama club. Those of us who do oral interp pick pieces like poems or monologues from a play. We memorize them, and then we perform them in competitions or shows."

"You want to memorize my poem?"

"Yeah."

"I don't know." Vera's brows furrow. "I wasn't even sure I wanted it published. It's pretty private."

Cecille looks disappointed. She picks out the last of her books and closes her locker. "If you don't want me to, I understand." She heads down the hallway.

Now it's time to plant a thought in Vera's head. "Let her do it. It must mean something to her if she wants to memorize it."

"Wait!" Vera calls out and jogs over to Cecille. "What would it sound like? I mean, how would you say it?"

"Why don't you come to drama club after school today? I could do a trial run in front of everyone. If it sounds good to you and them, then I'll work on memorizing it. If you don't like the way I read it or if the others don't approve, we'll skip it."

Vera bites her lip.

I whisper again. "It's better than going home to an empty house."

"Okay. I'll come."

"Great. Meet me in the auditorium right after school. I'll introduce you to everyone."

As Cecille walks off, Vera heads to lunch, the tiniest of smiles on her face.

The old excitement of the theater world calls to me throughout the rest of the day. I don't know how well Vera is concentrating, but all I can think about is drama club.

When I enter the auditorium with Vera at three o'clock, I have to whisper encouragement to get her to open the heavy doors and step inside. This is totally new territory for her, and it would take an idiot not to notice her trembling. I wonder if she's ever had any real friends before, or if she ever joined any activities at her middle school. Although I've been guarding her for months, I realize there's still much I don't know about her.

Vera stands at the back of the auditorium. High school kids are jumping over the fold-up, padded auditorium chairs or shuffling down the rows to get to their friends. Backpacks lay strewn everywhere. Snacks and bottles of Gatorade are consumed at a voracious rate — almost as fast as their mouths are chattering. Most of the kids sit in the first few rows, but a few have branched out to other spots in the auditorium.

A few more students enter from the doors behind Vera, who stands like a petrified tree; the latest arrivals nearly knock her over as they enter.

"Sorry," one of young girls calls as they hustle down the house left aisle.

Vera takes one step backwards.

"Stay right where you are, Vera Lavoy. Cecille wanted you to come." *Speaking of Cecille, where is she?* I scan the crowd. Cecille talks to Mr. Cardone down at the front. "Stay put," I tell Vera and fly over the heads of the other students.

I stop above Cecille in time to hear her say, "The poem was in the school literary magazine."

"You need permission from the poet," says Mr. Cardone.

"When we do a Shakespeare monologue, we don't have to get his permission."

"This is different. We're talking about a student here at our own school. Let's be courteous to our fellow artists."

"I told her to come after school, but I'm afraid she's chickened out."

I glide down over Cecille's shoulder. "Look up, Cecille. She's frightened. Welcome her."

"Oh wait. She's here. I'll go get her." Cecille dodges several other kids as she runs up the aisle.

At the top of the auditorium, Vera is clutching her bag so tightly she looks like someone fearing she's about to be robbed.

"Vera," my sister calls. "Come on. The meeting is about to start." God bless my sister. Without any encouragement from me, she practically drags Vera down the long aisle and brings her to a row with a couple of underclassman I don't recognize.

Two years have passed since my last drama club meeting so I only know about half the students. Gregory Hicks with his scraggly new beard runs the meeting so he must have been elected president. No surprise there. Shana Peters with her half-shaved head and all-black ensemble sits at the end of one row and whispers with her friend Lexy. All-around class clown Roger keeps interrupting Gregory from the back in what is obviously an attempt to impress the pretty blonde sitting next to him. I recognize a few others, but many are either underclassmen or upperclassmen who joined more recently. Mr. Cardone sits off to the side. As drama club moderator, he usually lets the club president run the meetings on his or her own and only steps in when there are problems or they need direction.

The first part of the meeting is spent practicing skits for the school's variety show, which is only a week and a half away. Watching their enthusiastic participation in the rehearsals reminds me of what I'm missing. I nearly slip into the darkness several times. I want to crawl into a corner, curl up into a ball and cry over what I've lost, the shows I'll never perform. But I can't fall into the darkness right now. I have to be here for Vera and my sister now.

Toward the end of the meeting, Gregory asks if anyone has something new they want to try. My sister jumps up.

"I've got a poem to read."

Vera tenses.

Cecille heads down the aisle. "I'm thinking I could use it as an oral interp piece for our next competition."

"Great," Gregory says. As my sister passes him on her way up the stage, he adds, "It's about time, little Dunston."

My sister rolls her eyes at him and takes the stage. In her hands is the literary magazine folded open to Vera's poem.

Back in her seat, Vera bites her lip as Cecille begins to read. My sister's voice is strong and reaches to the back corners of the auditorium. I wonder if she remembers the vocal exercises I used to do in my bedroom. She would always complain that I was being too loud and disturbing her homework, but I told her I had to be that loud so the little old deaf lady in the back of the auditorium could hear me.

Cecille's voice is so commanding that she has everyone's full attention right away and she holds it throughout the poem. Nobody shuffles in the seats; no one whispers to a neighbor. When she's done, there is silence for seconds that drag on.

Finally, Cecille breaks the silence. "So what do you guys think? Is it good for the oral interp comp?"

Shana Peters shouts from her seat on the far house left. "I've read that somewhere before."

Gregory Hicks says, "Is that the lit magazine you're holding?"

Cecille nods.

"Someone at *our* school wrote that?" asks a tall, gangly boy from the third row.

"Yeah," Cecille says. "In fact, she's sitting right over there."

Heads turn to where Cecille is pointing. Vera draws down into her seat.

"You wrote that?" asks a curly-haired brunette sitting in the same row.

Vera nods ever so slightly.

"That's really good," says the brunette.

"So should I do it for the competition or not?" asks Cecille.

"Let me see the poem again." Gregory stands up from his position in the orchestra pit and reaches for the magazine from my sister. He takes a moment to reread it as the other drama kids whisper. Vera looks like she wants to fall right through the auditorium floor.

"I like it," Gregory says, "but I feel like we could do more with it. See this part here?" He points to the final stanza. "This part is like the refrain of a song. Hold on." He heads over to the auditorium seats and pulls out a guitar case. I've forgotten he used to write little ditties for some of our skits. Gregory takes his guitar out of the case and strums a few chords. After a few tries, he finds a tune that is both mournful and reflective. Then he starts to sing, "I'm tired of being numb...I want to feel the light...I'm sick of looking at a world that's only black and white...Where did all the colors go?"

I forgot how amazing Gregory could be. He'd shown signs of talent the day he walked into drama club. Today he's proving why he's the leader of this group.

Several drama kids voice their approval of the song, and Vera looks like she's going to cry, but almost in a good way — like she's moved by Gregory's version of her own poem. There are no shadows nearby, so I can tell she's not upset by it. The only ones in the room who look a little worried are my sister and Mr. Cardone.

"Hold on a minute," says the drama club moderator. "Before you get too excited, we have a few things to consider." He looks to Vera. "First, we have to make sure we have the poet's permission to use the poem. She might not want us using her poem at all."

All eyes are on Vera.

Vera gives a little shrug. "I guess it's okay."

The curly-haired brunette two seats down smiles at her. Vera gives a small smile back.

"Next, this poem was brought up by Ms. Dunston as a piece for the oral interp competition."

"True," Gregory says, "but we've been looking for a song to add to the variety show skits."

Several students voice their agreement.

The curly-haired brunette jumps up from her seat. "Wait a second. You can't do that!" In that instant, I recognize her. She was friends with my sister back in middle school. Only she was about five inches shorter the last time I saw her, and she used to straighten her hair back then. But there's no doubt about the way she said, "You can't do that!" This is definitely Vicki Ramponni. "This is Cecille's piece to perform. You can't just take it away from her."

Everyone talks at once. It is clear that some of them side

with Vicki and others side with Gregory.

"Hold on!" Mr. Cardone waves his hands and jumps up on stage next to Cecille, who takes a seat on the lip of the stage. "Hold on, everyone! Maybe this doesn't have to be an either-or situation. Cecille could still use this as an oral interp piece next month at the competition. And if Vera is okay with it, Gregory could also work on it as an entry for the variety show."

More excited chatter.

"Gregory, can you finish the song in time?"

"I can have it done tonight."

Vicki stands with her arms folded. "I still think Cecille should be a part of the song if we perform it at the variety show. She's the one who brought it up."

Cecille shakes her head. "I don't want to sing it."

"Cece," Vicki calls my sister by her old nickname. Her voice is soft and coaxing now. "I wasn't thinking of you singing. You should *dance* to the song."

Immediately, I'm excited. My sister is a wonderful ballerina, and even from the little bit Gregory has played, and I can tell it would be perfect for a ballet, so I'm surprised by the sad look on my sister's face.

"Vicki, you know I can't do that. I haven't danced since…" She stops herself, and without her having to say anything, I somehow know she hasn't danced since my death. Time freezes for a moment. When I took my own life, I thought I'd be giving her the chance to attend the ballet school of her dreams. Instead, she stopped dancing completely.

Time restarts. The wind howls, and a shadow appears through the back doors. I fly to it.

"No," I tell the shadow. "You're not getting any farther than this." My wings are flung out behind me. I face the stage. "You can do this, Cecille. You can dance again. Don't give up as easily as I did."

My sister's voice is so small I can barely hear it from the other side of the auditorium. "I haven't danced in nearly two years."

Vicki leaves her seat and walks toward the stage. "Soooo? Who cares? You were an awesome dancer, and I'm sure you can do it again. Mr. Cardone, aren't you always saying we should try new things and not get stuck doing the same kinds of skits over and over again?"

I glance at the shadow swirling behind me as Mr. Cardone speaks from the stage. "Yes, it would be nice if the student body saw you guys as more than a comedy act. We should do some serious pieces, and we should include some music in our acts. If Mr. Hicks can compose the rest of the song tonight and get a copy to Ms. Dunston, I think this would be a great addition to our repertoire. The question is, can you get it done in time? The variety show is only nine days away."

"We can, Mr. Cardone," Gregory says. "I'll finish the song tonight. Then Cecille and I can work after school tomorrow on the dance. You cool with this, Little Dunston?"

Cecille nods, but I see the hesitation in her eyes.

Chapter Twenty-One

Another day passes and still no Warren or Ms. Kitchin. The rumor around school is that she's in the hospital. Some say it's a bad illness; others are talking suicide attempt. I worry about Warren. What happens to a Guardian if their Charge attempts suicide? Are they "dismissed" from the case? Are they given another chance?

After school, Cecille drags Vera back to the auditorium. "I want you there while we choreograph the piece. It's your poem after all."

"But I don't know anything about dance."

"You don't need to." Cecille pulls open the heavy auditorium door. "Listen. I'll give you my phone. I want you to record the dance while I practice. I've got a short time to learn whatever we choreograph, so having a video of it will help me practice at home in case I forget what we do at school."

Gregory's already inside the auditorium. He's on the stage arguing with Cathy Ringles, the snot-nosed captain of the dance team whose sister had died in that car accident. Behind her stands a bunch of girls, dressed in jazz pants and sequined tops.

"We had the auditorium booked weeks ago." Cathy has her hand thrown up in Gregory's face.

"Why can't you practice in the gym like you always do?"

"Because, Birdbrain, basketball season has started up again."

"But you've had plenty of chances to practice your dances. This is our first chance to practice ours."

"Yours? Don't tell me the theater geeks are going to try to dance?"

"Why shouldn't we?"

"And when are you going to perform this dance?"

"At the variety show."

"Oh, no way. The dance team already has two numbers entered into the variety show. That's our department. Why don't you guys stick to what you're good at? Stupid little skits that no one but you finds funny."

Cecille and Vera have slowly worked their way toward the stage. Vera looks like she wants to run out of there, but Cecille pulls at her elbow. As freshmen, I'm sure they don't want to get in the middle of this fight between two seniors, but that doesn't mean Cecille is about to walk away.

Mr. Cardone walks out from behind stage. "Hicks, come back to my classroom."

"But, Mr. Cardone—"

"You can use my classroom as rehearsal space."

Mr. Cardone's theater classes are held in a classroom that's designed like a black box theater. There's an open area at the front of the room that's maybe one-third the size of the real stage. Then there are several rows of desks on platforms that rise up like auditorium seats.

With an over-exaggerated sigh, Gregory grabs his backpack and his guitar. He spots Vera and my sister walking down the aisle and waves them to the back.

Gregory plays the song once all the way through for Vera, Cecille, and Mr. Cardone. Then he plays it again while Cecille ties on her toe shoes. When she is ready to start dancing, Cecille hands her phone over to Vera.

"Make sure you get my feet in the frame. The video won't do me any good if I can't see what my feet are doing."

Vera moves back a couple rows so she can get a better angle for filming.

For the next hour, all I do is marvel at my sister's dancing as Gregory plays the song over and over again. Sometimes she asks him to repeat a part while she works out some steps.

Other times, she has him stop completely while she works out some footwork. They start the song over and over again with Vera catching everything on video. After the first few run-throughs, Vera switches to the other side of the classroom and catches the dance from another angle.

In the back of the classroom, Mr. Cardone rifles through the costuming closet but every once in a while he makes a suggestion or breaks up an artistic disagreement between Cecille and Gregory.

From the smile on her face and the glow that emanates from her, I can tell my sister is happy to be dancing again. Vera smiles occasionally, but something is still troubling her.

When she heads home after the rehearsal, there is sadness in her eyes. And it doesn't take long after entering the house that the shadows fill the place. Once more, I am thrown into darkness.

I don't see the light again until Monday morning. Vera is at her locker, and my sister has just opened hers.

"I almost have the whole thing finished," Cecille says to Vera. "I must have watched the video like a hundred times this weekend." Her enthusiasm is contagious, and I can see Vera is happy for her, but the sadness lingers in her eyes.

"We've got another drama club meeting tomorrow after school. Can you come? Mr. Cardone said I can practice all I want on the stage after our regular rehearsal. If you could tape me again, that would be perfect. I think I'll really be able to spread the dance out — you know, fill the stage more — once I get to rehearse in the actual theater."

"Sure," Vera says.

"Great." Cecille slams her locker and heads off to class.

With Cecille so happy, I won't have to check on her today. I can spend the whole time with Vera. Something is clearly still wrong.

Class after class, I try to think of a way to help her. I mentally check off a list: I've already helped get her poem published, the poem is being performed not once, but twice, and she's been introduced to some new people. Maybe she'll finally make some friends.

At lunch, however, Vera still eats alone. I was hoping Gregory or Shana would notice her sitting at the loser's table, but that's too much to expect a senior to invite a freshman to their table.

Then I spot my sister's friend Vicki sitting with some other freshman girls at another table. A couple of the others are familiar from the drama club and one of them is even in Vera's English class. I fly over to Vicki.

"Invite Vera to sit here."

Vicki's eyes move around the cafeteria until she sees Vera sitting alone at the end of the loser's table.

She stands up. "I'll be right back, guys."

I want to giggle. It's almost too easy. Vera looks shocked when Vicki asks her to come sit with them, but she doesn't hesitate. One look at Ms. Eats-and-Pukes is enough to get Vera packing up her foil-covered lunch and heading on over.

I'm patting myself on the back all through lunch when I realize I'm still here. I'm not seeing whatever Betsy saw when she finished her assignment. While I may have gotten Vera some friends, I still haven't solved her problem.

That becomes all the more obvious when I follow Vera home. She isn't home more than ten minutes when she receives a text from her dad: "Working late again. Make yourself some dinner." And the darkness swallows us both.

On Tuesday, the rumors about Ms. Kitchin are not good.
"Yep, definitely in the hospital."
"This is like our fifth day with a sub."
"They found a suicide note in her condo."

"I heard she's in a coma."

Tuesday afternoon means drama club. Getting Vera into the seats is much easier this time with both Vicki and Cecille waving her in.

Vera laughs at the funny skits planned for the variety show on Friday night, but I can tell sadness hides behind a thin veneer. Besides, Friday night is the date circled on her calendar. The anniversary of her mother's death, and quite possibly the night Vera plans to die.

As Cecille dances, Vera once again records it on her phone. The dance is even more beautiful on the big stage. My baby sister's graceful steps and leaps take her from one side of the stage to the other. Her long, slender limbs reach farther than seems humanly possible, and on her toes, she is a delicate, long-stemmed rose reaching for the sun. Her movements are planned so that every time another color disappears in the song, her body contracts as if she can't handle the loss.

The heavy auditorium doors open and close so much that I don't think anyone but me notices when Cathy Ringles slips into the auditorium and sits down in a dark, back corner. Is it just me or does a dark, shadowy haze follow behind her? The dance team captain watches Cecille's rehearsal intently.

When the song ends, the rest of the drama kids applaud wildly. There's still work to be done, little kinks in the choreography and a couple stumbles in her footwork that need to be worked out, but it's clear from their reaction that everyone is impressed.

Cathy Ringles slips out the back quietly.

Vera, Cecille, and Gregory stay with Mr. Cardone to perfect the dance while the rest of the drama kids file out slowly.

Vera must be in a good mood after the rehearsal because the shadows aren't waiting for us when she returns home. As she makes herself some macaroni and cheese for dinner, I wonder if this performance will be enough for her to forget any thoughts of suicide. The only things that seem to be missing from her life are her mom (whose death I can do nothing about) and a real connection with her father (which I can't figure out how to make happen if the guy is never home when the house is shadow-free).

Before going to sleep, Vera pulls out a photo of her mom from her dresser. She places it next to her alarm clock. "I hope I'm making you proud, Mom." Her tiny voice barely escapes her lips. Her head falls on her pillow, and tears well up in her eyes.

I can hear the shadow howling through the house before I see it. When it enters the room, I am ready with my wings unfurled wide. "Leave," I tell it. "You won't take her into your darkness tonight." I'm facing the whirling storm cloud, so I turn my head over my shoulder and wings and call back to Vera, "You've had a good day, Vera. Don't let the darkness get to you. Look at what your poem has done. You got Gregory to write a song. You got my sister dancing again. I'm sure your mom must be proud of you."

The shadow continues to swirl and dance around Vera's room. I am there like a shield around Vera; anywhere the shadow moves, I move first. The minutes drag on while Vera cries into her pillow behind me and I shout encouragement over the howling wind. "Vera, you are talented. You have friends now. There is much to live for. Don't give in to the darkness. Fight it, Vera. Fight it!"

Eventually, Vera's sobs die down. She gasps a little for breath as the shadow finally retreats.

"Good girl, Vera. Don't let the monsters in." I'm weak from my fight with the shadow, but I won't let my wings relax until I'm sure the shadow is gone. A few minutes later, Vera's breathing has become steady, and she drifts off into sleep while I'm left to wonder how much longer I can keep fighting the shadows.

Chapter Twenty-Two

On Wednesday, I'm so confident of Cecille's happiness that I spend the entire day with Vera. It isn't until Vera packs her bag to go home that I realize Cecille isn't at her locker. I think Vera notices too because she keeps looking to her left like she's expecting Cecille to appear and invite her to another rehearsal at any moment.

Thinking maybe Cecille's already headed to the auditorium, I whisper to Vera, "Go to the theater anyway." Vera heads down the stairs. Gregory stands outside the auditorium.

"Gregory, do you know if Cecille is practicing today after school?"

"You didn't hear?" Gregory rubs his scraggly beard.

Vera shakes her head.

"She fell down the stairs before lunch. Twisted her ankle. There goes our musical piece for the variety show."

"Wait, what? How did it happen?"

Gregory shrugs. "Just clumsy, I guess."

Clumsy? How did my graceful ballerina of a sister suddenly turn clumsy?

"So you're not going to sing the song at the variety show?"

"It'd seem weird now without the dance." Gregory spots another senior boy from drama club over Vera's head. "Hey, Roger. Let's talk with Mr. Cardone about those changes in the Olympics skit."

"There in a minute," Roger calls back.

Gregory turns back to Vera. "Don't feel too bad, kiddo. We can always use the number for the spring arts festival." He gives Vera a little tap on the shoulder and enters the auditorium.

The spring arts festival? I can't wait that long. Vera's circled November 2 as the target date on her calendar. If my suspicions about that day are true, I only have three days left.

Vera simply stands there, clutching her bag and holding onto her coat like it's a security blanket. Other students move around her like a river flowing around a boulder. Eventually, the hallway empties. Students have either gone home or found their way to after-school activities.

When Vera lifts her head to look around, she seems startled by how empty the place has become. She sets down her bag and puts on her coat. After a glance toward the auditorium door, she heads out of the building.

My mind whirls. What on earth do I do now? *Oh God, help!* I have no idea what to do next. Vera must be devastated. My sister must be devastated. For a few moments, I think about going to check on her and leaving Vera to fend for herself, but I can't do that. Cecille is probably being taken care of by Mom. Vera will end up alone again. Still, the temptation is there. Cecille needs me, too.

When we get to Vera's home, the utter darkness inside tells me that the shadows are waiting for her. I throw myself in front of Vera's door.

"Don't go in, Vera. Go anywhere but here." I spread my wings wide, but Vera doesn't slow her steps. "There are too many memories of your mother inside and too much loneliness without your father home."

Vera plows right through me and into the house, and I am plunged into the darkness.

The darkness doesn't last long. Before I'm able to collect my thoughts, I hear a door slam shut at the back of the house, and I hurry around to see Vera stomping across the yard. She has left the bag in her house and is headed for the detached garage. In her hand, she clutches her phone and studies a map she's pulled up on it.

Vera unlocks the side door of the garage and steps inside. Within seconds, the large garage door opens, and Vera pulls out an old girl's bicycle. Parking it on the driveway, she closes the garage door behind her and takes one last look at the map on the phone before shoving it in her pocket and hopping on her bike.

I have no idea where she's headed. Her path seems to take us back to the school, but she rides past the turn that would take us there. As I follow her, I'm glad my wings are fully functioning now. With the way she's pedaling, I never could have caught up with her before my wings grew.

I wonder if she's riding hard just to burn off anger and frustration, but then I remember the map, and I know there's a purpose to her trip. My next thought is that she's looking for the cemetery her mother's buried in, but after a few more turns, the streets become more and more familiar. With the final turn onto Chestnut, my heart begins to ache. I know exactly where she's going, but I don't know if I can handle going with her.

The sight of my house splits my heart in two. Why did it never look so pretty when I was alive? It doesn't matter that it's fall now, and the trees are all bare. The little front porch on our farm-style home is so welcoming I want to cry out in agony. Why didn't I appreciate it when I was alive? Once again, I am reminded of Emily Webb's words, "Oh, earth, you are too wonderful for anybody to realize you."

Vera flips down the kickstand after dragging the bike up the little path that leads to the porch. She double-checks the address on her phone before ringing the bell. I hear every little sound in the next few seconds. The squirrel scratching its way up a nearby tree. The breeze blowing some dead leaves across the sidewalk. The muffled sound of padded slippers making their way to the front door. Vera rubs her arm as a cool breeze passes by. With a squeak, the door opens, and I see my mother close-up for the first time since my death.

"Oh, Mama!" I moan. She looks so thin, so frail, and she wears a scarf to hide the chemo-induced baldness. I don't want to look. I pray that God won't make me look, but I have to. I have to protect both Vera and Cecille now.

"Can I help you?" my mother asks.

"I'm here to see Cecille. I really need to see Cecille." Vera blurts out the words like she's afraid if she doesn't get the words out fast she'll lose any confidence she has.

"Are you a friend?" Mom narrows her eyes.

Again the words tumble out one after the other. "I'm in the drama club with her. We were working on a number for Friday night's show, and when I showed up for rehearsal after school, I heard she got hurt."

"That's right."

"Is she okay?"

"Her ankle is twisted pretty badly."

"Can I see her?"

I can tell my mom is studying this girl with the flushed face, the wind-blown hair, and thrift-store jacket. She is not the well-put-together type my sister usually hangs out with.

"I don't know...the painkillers the doctors gave her made her pretty woozy."

"Please," Vera begs. "Tell her I've got a plan for us to save the number." Another cool wind blows and Vera rubs her arm to fight off the shivers.

"Why don't you wait inside? I'll go see how she's feeling." Mom opens the door, and Vera steps inside. "I'll be back in just a moment."

Vera surveys the living room. The inside of my house hasn't changed since the day I died, but that doesn't make it any easier for me to see. Near the front picture window is where I waited for Billy Michaels to pick me up for my first school dance. On the mantel above the fireplace are pictures of Cecille and me taken over the years at school. On the end table is the purple vase I'd made in ceramics class. My mother's favorite cooking magazine rests on the coffee table. It simultaneously feels like just yesterday and a million years ago that I last stood in this room.

I'm actually relieved when my mom shuffles back into the room and tells Vera that my sister is sleeping. I can't look at my house without being reminded of how much I loved it.

"Could you give Cecille a message for me?" Vera begs as my mom shows her to the door. "Could you tell her to call me or text me?" Vera pulls a piece of paper from her pocket. "Here's my number."

My mom takes the slip. "I'll let her know you stopped by," she says as she closes the door on Vera.

Outside the house I feel like I can breathe again, but Vera is clearly devastated. She slowly gets back on the bike and pedals home. I don't know if Cecille calls her later because I'm thrown into darkness as soon as I follow Vera into the house.

Cecille is back at school the next day, but she's on crutches and wearing an ankle boot. As soon as Vera sees her hobble down the hallway, she runs up to her.

"What happened? I went to your house yesterday, but your mom said you were sleeping. I gave her my number but you never called."

"Sorry," Cecille's eyes are cast down.

"Listen, it doesn't matter. I've got a way we can still perform the song."

Cecille rests her crutches against the row of lockers and slides the backpack off her shoulders. "In case you haven't noticed, Vera, I'm not exactly in a position to dance."

"You don't have to dance tomorrow night. You've already done the dance."

Cecille looks at her. "Huh?"

"We've got it all in your phone."

"What good does that do?" Cecille starts unpacking her bag while Vera chatters excitedly beside her.

"It does all the good in the world. Listen, here's my plan. You send the videos from your phone to my email. I'll edit the footage from the different rehearsals together and make like a multimedia kind of presentation with it. You know, sort of a music video. Gregory can perform the music live while the video is playing on the big screen in the auditorium."

"It won't be the same."

"You're right, it won't." Vera's shoulders slump. "But it could still be really good. I mean, you did such a great job with the dance. People should get to see it."

The two girls are silent while Cecille arranges the last of the books and hoists her bag onto her shoulders.

"How did you fall anyway?"

"I didn't fall. I was tripped."

"What?"

"Cathy Ringles was headed up the stairs when I was headed down to lunch. My arms were full of books because I had stuff to drop off at the library. Cathy stuck her foot where I couldn't see it behind all the books, and I tripped. Next thing I knew I'd fallen four stairs to the landing."

"She did it on purpose." Vera's words aren't a question.

"Yeah, I think so." Cecille sighs and picks up her crutches.

"Did you tell anyone?"

"I told the school nurse who brought in Principal Rainer. He told me he'd 'investigate'." Cecille squeezes the crutches under her elbows in order to do the air quotes.

"So did he?"

"When my mom called the school after I got home from the doctor, Principal Rainer said Cathy Ringles told him I must've tripped on my own two feet, and none of the kids who were in the stairwell at the time saw anything."

The warning bell rings.

"I've got to get to class," Cecille mutters.

"What about the video idea?"

"I'll think about it." She hobbles off in one direction as Vera heads in the other.

I no longer expect to see Warren or Ms. Kitchin in English class. The students don't seem surprised by her absence either. No one whispers when Mr. Carter walks in for the umpteenth day in a row.

At lunch I'm not surprised when Vera sits at the table with Vicki and her friends since she's been eating there all week, but I nearly fall over when Vera gets up from the table and heads to a different one. In her hand she carries a copy of the literary magazine. It's folded open to her poem and the student drawing that was picked out to run alongside it.

"Excuse me," Vera says to a boy several tables away from her own. He's wearing an oversized basketball jersey, but that doesn't stop his boxers from showing over a pair of jeans worn way too low. I've seen him before. Must be in one of her classes. "You're Hugo Vasquez, aren't you?" Her voice squeaks, and she swallows hard.

He glances at her briefly before saying, "Why do you want to know?"

"I like your drawing." Vera holds out the magazine.

Hugo's eyes flicker to the magazine and then Vera. "So?"

"So I want your permission to include it in a video I'm...the drama club is making."

"What kind of video?" Hugo chomps on a few cafeteria fries.

"The drama club is doing this whole thing with the poem

I wrote. It's going to be part of a video shown at the variety show tomorrow night, and I think it'd be cool to show your artwork in the video."

Hugo looks at Vera for the first time like he's really seeing her. "You wrote that poem?"

Vera nods.

Hugo goes back to his fries. "What do I get if I let you put my drawing in the video?"

"Fame?" She gives a sheepish grin.

Hugo snorts. "They won't even know who did the drawings."

"I'll put in a special 'artwork by' section at the end of the video."

A boy on the other side jumps into the conversation. "You should do it, Hugie. Give her those other ones you did, too."

"You have other drawings?"

Hugo lifts a shoulder. "I got some other stuff the magazine people didn't use."

"Do they match my poem? 'Cause this whole video's kind of built around the poem."

"Yeah, I tried out a couple ideas after reading your poem."

"Could I take pictures of them?" The growing excitement can be heard in her voice.

"I'll be in the art studio after school. You can come by then."

Vera does a little happy jump.

"You better be quick. I'm not stickin' around forever waiting for you."

"I'll be there right away."

I'm worried Vera has put the cart before the horse. Adding Hugo's drawings is a great idea, and I'm shocked by how willing she was to approach a guy she didn't know, but none of it's going to be any good if my sister doesn't send her the video.

The next time I see Cecille she's fuming. Vera is packing up her bag and ready to rush down to the art studio when Cecille comes hobbling up.

"You were right, Vera." She sets her crutches against the wall. "Cathy did trip me on purpose."

"You have proof?"

"Not exactly. I just passed by Cathy's locker. She was there with a couple of dance team girls, and when she saw me, she gave me this totally fake, 'Oh, how sad! Now you won't be able to dance tomorrow night!' And the girls next to her started giggling."

Vera lifts her bag from the floor. "You can't let her get away with this."

"What can I do? It's her word against mine."

"Send me the videos off your phone. I've got this whole plan. Listen, I've got to go. I promised someone I'd meet him." Vera heads away. "Just send me the video. I'll take care of everything."

Vera means what she says. In the art studio, Hugo lets her take photos of several of his pieces that he had made based on her poem. Then he shows her some mixed media work he did, and Vera snaps more photos. A number of his pieces are focused on single colors, like a collage of pieces that are all yellow: photos of daffodils, pieces of yellow yarn, cut-up sections of yellow cereal boxes.

When she finishes with Hugo, Vera runs to Mr. Cardone's room. He's still there grading papers when Vera dashes in and spills her plan. I marvel at how smart she is being. Where did this girl come from? You give her an ounce of confidence, and she runs with it.

In fact, by the time Vera is home and working on the

video, mixing clips of Cecille's dance with photos of Hugo's artwork, I'm wondering why I'm not moving on yet. This girl is way too excited to be suicidal. Perhaps God hasn't called me to sainthood yet because He needs me to help my sister. Maybe I'm not here for Vera anymore. Maybe I'm here for Cecille.

I wish Warren had been at school today. I could really use his advice. Maybe I should fly over to my old house to check on Cecille. No, I don't think I'd last long in there. The memories of what I've left behind are too painful for me. I resolve to simply wait and see what tomorrow brings.

Chapter Twenty-Three

By third period on Friday, Vera is ridiculously excited about the variety show, and although Cecille would rather be dancing the song live, she seems okay with Vera's video. So why haven't I passed on to sainthood?

There's only one person I want to ask. I make one last check on Vera in English and Cecille in French class before I fly out of school. Our neighborhood has only one hospital so knowing where to go isn't hard. The difficult part is knowing which room is Ms. Kitchin's. I skip the children's section and the emergency room. After that, it's mostly random guessing.

"Do you need help?"

It takes me a moment to realize the voice is speaking to me. A dark-skinned woman in a white nurse's outfit glides right through the half wall that surrounds the nurse's station on the third floor. The crests of her angel wings peek out over her shoulders. She smiles radiantly, and I have a sudden vision of her singing in a Gospel choir.

"I'm looking for someone. A Guardian."

"We have many here." Her eyes sparkle as she tilts her head at me.

As soon as she says it, I realize how many winged souls are guiding patients, nurses, and doctors down the hall. I was so intent on finding Ms. Kitchin — and thereby finding Warren — that I hadn't even bothered looking at who else was here.

"I'm looking for one named Warren."

"Perhaps if you tell me who he's guarding. I'm afraid I'm really better with the patients' names."

"Ms. Kitchin. I don't know her first name."

"Oh yes, the teacher. Well, I'm afraid I don't know anything about her having a Guardian."

"What do you mean?"

"According to her records, she was found in a church in Springville with a terrible gash in her head like she'd had a bad fall." The nurse shakes her head and gives a quiet cluck. "Terrible concussion, the poor thing. Everyone thought it was just an accident until they found a suicide note in her purse. She's been pretty out of it ever since. Keeps muttering that she needs to get back to her kids, but her medical records say she never had any."

I know the medical records won't show the baby she had on her own, but I decide not to tell the Guardian Nurse that she had abandoned Warren in a church.

"So you haven't seen a Guardian named Warren around her?"

"No, sorry."

"Could you tell me where Ms. Kitchin is? Even if I can't see Warren, I'd like to see how she's doing."

"Sure thing, sugar. Down the hall and then left. Room 314."

The room has two beds in it, but only the far one is occupied. I barely recognize Ms. Kitchin. Her head is bandaged, and she's not wearing any make-up. An empty chair sits next to the window, and I hope beyond hope that Warren will suddenly appear.

As I wait, I think about what the Guardian Nurse said, that Ms. Kitchin kept talking about getting back to her kids. And I think about what Warren had said about Ms. Kitchin trying to find out what happened to him. Had she found out he died, so she attempted suicide? Is Warren really gone for good because he failed?

Minutes tick by. Nurses come in and out checking on Ms. Kitchin, taking her temperature, reviewing her chart.

At one point, Ms. Kitchin stirs. "Need to get back," she mutters. "Need to help...kids."

"Ms. Kitchin," I rise from my chair. "There are students who need your help. Vera needs you. I've been trying to help her, but I don't know what else to do. You were right about her poem. Everyone loves it, but she needs more. She needs…" And then it's all so clear, as if the picture's finally come into focus. "She needs a father who is as desperate to know her and love her as you were desperate to know and love your son Warren. If only Vera's dad knew what he was missing by not spending time with her."

The words are barely out of my mouth when I realize what I must do. When I check the clock on the wall, I'm startled by how much time has passed.

I catch up with Vera as she's walking home. The good news is that the house seems free of shadows. The bad news is that her father is absent again.

Vera makes herself a quick dinner and then watches the video she's made two more times. Before leaving the house, she writes a note to her dad and leaves it on the kitchen table:

"Dad,

I'm at school for the variety show. If you get this message on time, please come to the high school. I wrote a poem, and one of the drama club members made it into a song. It's being performed tonight. Show starts at 8:00.

Vera."

Then she grabs her bag and heads back to school.

Cecille is backstage with the rest of the performers. It's hard not to get caught up in the excitement before a show. Costumes are donned. Make-up is applied. Lines are run, and dance steps are perfected. My heart aches with the loneliness I feel. All the nervous performers have someone else to confide in. I have no one to tell how much I miss it all.

Before the show begins, Vera peeks out at the audience. I know what she wants to see, but her father isn't there. I mentally berate myself for not paying more attention to

173

where her dad works. If only he could see this video, maybe he'd know how much his daughter needs him.

Vera sighs and walks backstage. She pulls out her phone and checks for messages.

The phone! I fly out of the school and back down the streets to Vera's house. Her dad still isn't home; the message on the kitchen table is untouched, but that doesn't matter for my plan. Luckily, I've watched Vera log onto her computer enough times that I know all her passwords. I pull up the video and send it to her dad's phone with a brief message: "Variety Show at school tonight. This is my video and song."

He might not make it to the show, but I'm not going to let this night pass without him seeing what his daughter has been working on. I say a prayer as I hit send. "Please, God, help this man to see how much his daughter needs him."

As I head out the door, I pass by a calendar. It stops me cold. How had I not noticed how quickly the last few days had passed? Today's date is circled on the calendar. It's November 2, the day Vera plans to take her life.

The variety show is well under way by the time I return. Bands play, the drama club performs, the dance team dances, and the singers soar. Vera's video is scheduled for the end of the show.

Vera and I both peek out at the audience to see if her dad has shown up. The auditorium is almost full, and the people out there whoop and holler for their favorite acts. I recognize a few faces from Vera's classes or the cafeteria, and my mom sits in a back row by herself. I wonder if she even told Dad about tonight. I continue to scan the crowd for Vera's dad, but I end up finding my own father on the opposite side of the auditorium far from my mother.

It's the first time I've seen him since my death, and I don't know how to feel. I'm glad he's here to support Cecille, but at the same time, I'm angry. He never really supported my dream of a life in the theater. I think part of him was actually happy when DePaul rejected me.

"Keep the door closed, Ms. Lavoy." Mr. Cardone stands on the steps behind us. "You're letting the light from the backstage area into the auditorium. We want that dark."

Vera quickly closes the door. "Sorry."

"Your video all set to go?"

"I downloaded it on the computer for the stage manager. He said he'd have it all cued and ready to go."

"Good." Mr. Cardone heads back to his classroom where the other acts are watching the current performance on closed-circuit TV. I thought Vera might do the same thing, but instead she walks to the stage right wing where Gregory holds his guitar.

"You ready?" she whispers.

Gregory nods. The audience bursts into cheers as the dance team finishes up a routine full of acrobatic lifts and jumps. After a quick bow, they rush off the stage, their cheeks flushed.

Cathy Ringles pauses on her way off stage. "Good luck, Gregory. Too bad the dancing isn't live. It's so much more impressive that way."

If I were still alive, I would have socked her in the nose.

She saunters off, and Gregory turns to Vera with a smile. "Too bad their music was canned. It's so much more impressive when it's a live musician."

Vera giggles as a soft thumping is heard behind us. Cecille is hobbling her way over as the emcee for the show picks up his mic.

"For our next act, we are combining the talents of several student artists. It all began with a poem written by Vera Lavoy. Hugo Vasquez drew several amazing pieces of art based on the poem, and Drama Club President Gregory

Hicks turned the poem into a song, which Cecille Dunston danced to. It all comes together in our next act. Singing 'Colors,' please welcome Gregory Hicks."

Gregory strolls out onto the stage, his guitar in one hand and a three-legged stool in another. Behind him a large screen is lowered. The lights lower as Gregory sets the stool behind a mic on stage right.

"This song is for all those times when things don't go our way, and we feel like the world is disappearing on us."

In the hush of the theater, Gregory strums his guitar as the video begins behind him. From our angle backstage, we get a slanted view of the picture, but it's clear how well Vera has blended the footage of Cecille's dancing with Hugo's artwork. To make it even more amazing, Vera has edited the footage so that the colors literally disappear from the video. Once Gregory sings about yellow disappearing, no more yellow appears in the video. Once he sings about red going, there's no more red anywhere. By the time he gets to blue disappearing, we're watching black and white footage.

"Awesome," Cecille whispers under her breath.

As Gregory plays the last few chords of the song, the screen goes black and then printed in white appear the words "Waiting for the rainbow after the rain."

The final chord lingers in the air. The audience is silent. Vera looks like she's unable to breathe. And then the audience bursts into applause. Gregory bows and steps off the stage, carrying the stool and his guitar with him. He stops by Cecille and Vera in the wings.

"Good job," Cecille says.

"You too," he says.

She smiles sheepishly. "I didn't do anything."

"Yeah, ya did. You created an awesome dance, and you brought the poem to us."

"Yeah, but Vera wrote it."

"True."

Vera blushes. "Thanks."

On stage, the emcee introduces the final band of the night. They are a loud rock band that has everyone on their feet before the show ends.

When it's all over, Cecille drags Vera out to meet our mother. I decide to hang back. It hurts too much to be near her. The pain of missing my old life — the one I so recklessly threw away — is more than I can bear.

Even from this distance, I can tell Vera is a little embarrassed by how much my mother is congratulating her on the video. She's also a little distracted. She's trying to look like she's paying attention to my sister and mother, but she keeps sneaking glances around the auditorium.

My sister follows her gaze, but her eyes stop on our dad. He looks old and sad. He gives a little nod to Cecille.

"Dad's here," Cecile says.

Mom's eyes follow Cecille's. "I called him this afternoon and told him it would mean a lot to you if he could make it."

Cecille smiles. "Thanks, Mom. I think I'll go talk to him."

I'm happy for Cecille, but Vera looks crushed. Her dad didn't show.

Watching Cecille head over to our father is too much for Vera. She says goodbye to my mom, grabs her coat and bag from backstage, and heads toward the exit. There's still a lot of people taking off make-up or putting away instruments. Many of them compliment Vera as she passes, but she pays little attention.

I hear the shadow howling as soon as we approach the door. Tamesis is waiting for Vera outside. My wings unfurl instantly.

"Stay back," I growl. "She's worked too hard for tonight. Don't you dare ruin it for her." Then I turn and address Vera as she heads down the street. "Be proud of yourself, Vera.

You did well tonight. You helped my sister, and everyone loved your song and video. So your dad wasn't there. So what? Maybe he was working late again. He does have to pay the bills."

Even as I say it, I don't believe it. Things only get worse as we approach the house. Storm clouds roll in, and with them comes a multitude of shadows. Tamesis has apparently called on a slew of her deathly friends for help. They encircle us and draw closer to Vera. Tamesis is the only one whose face can be clearly seen. Most of them are just faceless cloaked figures. I beat them back with my wings. I've never seen so many shadows attack one person at a time.

A drop falls onto Vera's cheek. At first, I'm not sure if it's a tear or rain. A moment later, raindrops begin to mark up the sidewalk. The gray clouds above are unleashing their heavy load. Vera pulls up her hood, but it doesn't cover her face. Soon raindrops blend with the tears streaming down her cheeks.

"Don't give up, Vera," I shout over the howl of the wind. The shadows creep closer, forming a tighter circle around us. "No," I yell at them. Darkened faces form within the shadows. Tamesis's many reinforcements are quickly feeding off Vera's despair. I try to see through them to the houses. How much farther do we have to go to get home?

I can barely make out where we are until we pass a red truck in a driveway. I've seen it many times before, and I know that means we are only a few houses away from home. But will home do us any good? It's never protected us from the shadows before.

The wind picks up even more. I feel like we are caught in the vortex of a hurricane. An even darker shadow makes its way through the crowd of skull-faced shadows. This one, however, has a face of flame and eyes that glow electric blue.

"Belphagor!" I spit out his distasteful name.

"You have failed, Nanette." His fiery breath scorches my face.

"No!"

"Yes. Look at her. Vera has given up. She's had this date picked out for a while. Tonight will be the night she takes her own life."

"I won't let her."

"You can't stop her. God gave her free will just like he gave you." Belphagor flicks out one of his tongues of flame and licks the edge of his lips.

Tamesis moves alongside Belphagor and stretches out a bony hand toward Vera. "Mine," moans Tamesis.

I move in front and deflect her hand with a flick of my wings.

Tamesis withdraws her hand with a hiss like she's just been burned. Her face is more fully formed than I've ever seen it before. She looks less like a shadowy cloud and more like a teenage girl.

"Tammy." The name falls from my lips with the sudden recognition. This is Cathy Ringles's older sister who died in a car crash.

"I am not Tammy anymore!"

"You *were* Tammy. You died when you car went flying off the bridge during that ice storm. Your family blamed the construction crew that was rebuilding the bridge." And then I see what's really been going on. "The construction crew that was headed by Vera's dad."

"I am not Tammy," she shouts again.

"You're trying to get revenge for your death."

Belphagor flies between me and Tamesis. "Enough! You've failed in your mission, Nanette. It is time to see that the God you've placed your trust in has deserted you."

I shake my head. "No."

I don't want to give in to Belphagor, but my hopes sink

179

when we reach the house. Lights are on inside the house. Vera's dad is definitely home, which means he must have seen Vera's note and actually chose not to go to the show.

"See?" Belphagor taunts. "There is Vera's father, sitting inside watching television. He doesn't care for his daughter. He's ignored the message you sent him. Just like God is ignoring you."

"No." I shake my head. I'm face to face with Belphagor. His blue eyes burn hotter than his flaming skin. They pierce my soul, but I refuse to back down. "You can't have me."

I fly to Tamesis whose skeletal face is inches from Vera's. I push her back.

"And you can't have *her*." I curve my wings protectively around Vera.

Tamesis opens her mouth to let out a frustrated scream, and I see the worms and maggots making their way in and out the open sockets of her skull. I leave her and fly around the circle of demon shadows that entrap Vera.

"None of you can have her!"

In protest, the shadows rise up, row after row, until they form an ever-widening tower above us. As one, they spin in formation. They are a hurricane howling around Vera, who stands as if frozen in the eye of the storm. Can she sense the shadows around her?

I fly up in a spiral inside the shadow hurricane. "You can't have either of us. We don't belong to you. Do you hear me?"

As I fly past, inching my way up the hurricane, I see the death and decay in what little remains of their souls. The primordial ooze drips from their jaws as the parasites worm their way through the peaks and valleys of their skulls.

"Do you understand?" I scream over their moaning and chanting. "I will not let you take her."

In reply, the shadows wail as they spin a vortex around

us. The sound of hundreds of angry shadows is unlike anything I've heard before. Part howling wind, party agonizing cry, their piercing wails fill my senses. The noise they make is pure anger and agony with the volume cranked to the limit.

Belphagor and Tamesis are mixed up in the swirl of shadows. I can only tell where Belphagor is when his bright blue eyes whizz past me.

"WE. DO NOT. BELONG. TO. YOU!" I look up, behind the top row of shadows that spin around us. In the center above our heads is a patch of blue sky. How is it possible? A bit of blue sky on a stormy night?

I'm hit with a memory of my first training session with Warren. *God is like the sun — even on the stormy days when we cannot see Him, He still shines on the other side of the clouds.*

The shadows swirl around me so fast, I must beat my wings furiously to keep from being swept up with them.

"We do not belong to the darkness. We belong to the light!" I lift my hand up and stretch toward the patch of blue sky. No sooner do I reach up, than a shaft of blinding light pours from the sky into the eye of the storm. The shadows recoil, screaming in agony. The light bursts like an exploding sun. I struggle to remain airborne, but my wings fail, and I'm knocked to the ground before I know it.

The wind dies.

The rain stops.

The shadows have all fled.

Vera stands on the walk leading up to her front door. The storm is over, but she's soaked, her mousy brown ponytail dripping down her back. She seems frozen, as if terrified to move forward. Does she have any idea of the battle I've just fought for her?

I fly before her, standing between her and the front door. "Vera, you've got to do what I didn't. You've got to ask for help. Talk with your dad. He must be hurting after your mother's death, too. Just ask for your father's help, Vera. It's not too late."

Vera takes in a deep breath, and the words fall out of her mouth, not more than whisper. "Please, God."

She steps right through me and opens the front door.

"You're home," her father says as soon as she walks in. He's sitting on the recliner in the living room. "Come in here."

Vera walks in and sits down on the couch opposite him. Her eyes are cast down, and her hands are clasped on top of her knees.

"How'd it go tonight?"

"You saw my note?"

"Yeah."

Vera plays with her fingers. "Why didn't you come?"

"Who said I didn't?"

Vera looks up. "I looked around. You weren't there."

"Not in the audience."

"I don't understand."

Mr. Lavoy grins. The expression looks odd on his face. I've only seen him grumpy. He actually looks happy. How can that be when his daughter is in so much agony? "Principal Rainer and I were classmates at good old Worthington High. Used to work the spotlights together for all the shows. When he saw me tonight, he brought me upstairs to brag about all the new equipment they got." Mr. Lavoy whistles. "Man, that's some fancy technology you kids got now."

"You were up in the lighting booth?"

"Yep."

"Why didn't you stick around after the show?"

His smile fades. "Had to leave right after your video."

"You hated it that much?"

"No." Frown lines appear on his face. "No, I didn't hate it. I had to leave because I realized how much I've messed up."

"What do you mean?"

"Honey, you're not the only one who's lost all the color in her world since your mother died."

Vera's lip quivers.

Her dad looks her straight in the eye. "I should've been there for you. We should have been there for each other."

The last thing I see is Vera standing up and reaching out her arms for her father.

And then my whole world goes white.

Chapter Twenty-Four

The white light is warmth turned into color. Or rather all colors. Isn't that what they taught us in school? That black is the absence of color, and white is the combination of all colors.

A familiar voice calls to me. "Congratulations, Nanette. You've finished your angelhood."

Slowly a shape forms before my eyes.

"Warren?"

He smiles. "You did an excellent job." His white collared shirt and dress pants make him blend into his surroundings.

"I'm finished?"

"Yes."

"And you made it too? Ms. Kitchin didn't attempt suicide?"

"No. She found out the truth about me, and then she wept for a long time. She was thinking of taking her own life, but she went to the church where she left me and prayed that God would forgive her. She promised to rededicate her life to her students if that's what God wanted."

"Then how did she get hurt?"

"A few kids from the neighborhood snuck into the church, knocked her over the head, and took the cash out of her wallet. She was so deep in prayer, she didn't hear them coming."

"Is she going to be all right?"

"She'll be fine. In fact, I hear she's about to meet a very handsome doctor." Warren smiles.

I look around. All I see is white still.

"So, what now?"

"It's time to go home."

"Home." The word feels funny to say. I know home

means heaven and God, and sainthood was all I'd been hoping for since learning I was assigned a Guardianship, but something feels off.

"Betsy talked of home when she saw the light, too." I stop for a moment. "I don't mean to sound ungrateful, but I always thought I'd feel happy about it like she did."

Warren clasps his hands behind his back. "Do you miss your old home?"

I can't stop the tears before they fall. "I was so stupid, Warren. Why did I give it all up? I could have done so much more with my life. I could have been there for my sister...and my mother...and," I consider Vera and her dad, "maybe even my dad. I didn't appreciate what I had. I even thought I was doing them some good when I died. I thought Cecille would go to ballet school. I thought I'd save them from pain."

I wipe away the tears and look up. Warren is gone, and I am surrounded only by white again.

I can't tell which way is up and which way is down, but I suddenly have the sensation of lying on my back. A middle-aged man with a graying beard appears on my right as if he were standing next to a bed I was lying on. He is dressed all in white like Warren was, but I can't see any wings behind him.

He speaks, but most of his words sound like gibberish to me. Finally, I make out the word "name" among the foreign sounding ones.

"Name?" I say.

"Yes," he speaks clearly now in English. "Can you tell me your name?"

"Nanette."

The man holds up a clipboard and checks something off. "Last name?"

"Dunston."

He nods. "What date is it, Nanette?"

Date? What in heaven's name does he want to know that for? I want to ask him what is going on, but I fear if I answer the question wrong, they won't let me past the pearly gates, which I'm sure must be just beyond my sight.

I wrack my brain for the date. Images of Vera surrounded by the death shadows haunt me. Then I recall her and her father in the living room. The date was important. It had been circled on calendars.

"November 2," I reply. Or is it the third? How much time has passed?

The man with the beard frowns and walks away.

"Wait!" I call, but he's gone, and I'm surrounded only by white again.

Moments pass. Will the man return? Will Warren?

Another face appears, this time on my left.

"I know you," I call out, thankful to have another soul present. The woman smiles at me and takes my hand. She is the Guardian Nurse who'd helped me find Ms. Kitchin in the hospital. Her luminescent wings shimmer behind her.

"Hello, babydoll." She gently squeezes my hand.

"What's going on?"

"You're almost there, sugar. Hang on." She presses two fingers against my wrist like she's taking my pulse.

"Almost where?" I ask. "Home?"

She smiles at me. "Yes, baby. You'll be home soon." She gives my hand another squeeze and then fades into the background.

"No!" I cry out. "Don't go. Don't leave me here alone. I'm frightened."

Her wings shimmer in the distance, and then my world returns to white.

More time passes.

I don't know how long I stay in the whiteness, but

eventually I hear another familiar voice call to me.

"Nanette, Nanette, can you hear me? Mom, come quick, I think her eyelids fluttered."

I struggle to focus on the image before me. Cecille is on my right. My mother on my left. I must be lying down. On a bed maybe. The ceiling is white.

"Honey, can you hear us?" My mother's voice is soft. She does not wear a headscarf. Her hair looks as I remember it.

On my right, Cecille comes into focus. Her hair is long, and she looks twelve again. She looks like she did when I was alive.

Alive.

The thought lingers as my mother and sister whisper soothing words.

"It's all right, sweetie. You're in the hospital, but everything's fine now."

In the background, a machine beeps regularly, marking the passage of time.

Cecille raises a hand to her face and wipes away a tear. Could it be? Am I alive again? Or are we all dead, and this is heaven?

I must speak.

The words don't want to come at first. My lips barely move.

"What…"

"It's okay, honey."

"No, Mom. Let her speak."

"What…happened?"

Mom and Cecille exchange concerned looks.

"You don't remember?" Cecille asks.

I lick my parched lips.

"Give her some water, Cece."

My sister grabs a nearby cup and holds a straw to my lips. I feel like I've never tasted water before, but I can only swallow so much.

I release the straw. "I shot myself."

Another look between Mom and Cecille.

"Why am I not dead?"

The corner of Cecille's mouth turns up in the slightest of smiles. "Because you have terrible aim."

I raise an eyebrow. Or at least I think I do. It's hard to tell right now.

My mom leans in close. "The bullet didn't go straight into your head. It fired at more of an angle and skimmed your skull. You lost a lot of blood. You were in a coma, and you've slowly been coming out of it. Do you remember anything from the past couple weeks?"

I shake my head. A couple of weeks? I thought nearly two years had passed. I was with Vera for at least a month.

Mom's face is only a foot or so from mine. I lift my hand. I have to touch her to know she's real. I reach up and brush my fingers against her golden hair.

"Not a wig," I say.

Mom draws back in surprise. "Of course not. Why would I be wearing a wig?"

"You don't have cancer?"

"No." Eyebrows furrow.

"What about Aunt Tippy?"

"What do you mean?" asks Cecille.

"Does she have breast cancer?"

Both of them stand with their mouths open. Finally, my mom says, "She was diagnosed two days ago. How did you know?"

I swallow. "Just a funny dream."

"Maybe you are remembering things you heard us say during the coma," my mom suggests.

"Have you been tested recently?" I ask her.

"For what?"

"Breast cancer?"

"No."

"Get tested," I say.

"Oh, honey, I'm sure I'm fine."

I shake my head. "You need to get tested."

"Nanette—"

"You had stage four breast cancer in my dream."

Cecille's eyes are wide. "What about me? Was I in your dream?"

"Yes," I say, "and you were perfect. Don't change a thing. Keep dancing." I lift my head a bit and look around the hospital room. "Where's Dad?"

My mother bites her lip before responding, "He hasn't been around much. He was the one who found your note. He figured even if—when—you came out of the coma, you wouldn't want to see him. Nanette, he feels terrible about not supporting your dreams."

"Can you call him? I want to talk with him."

My mother nods. "I'll call him right now." She grabs her purse from the chair and pulls out the phone. "I should probably let the doctors and nurses know how alert you are." She heads for the hallway. Cecille and I are alone in the room.

"I am so sorry, Cece."

"For what, Nan?"

"For everything. For not being there for you. For letting you find me...like that. No sister should have to see that."

The tears well up in Cecille's eyes again. "I thought I'd lost you for good."

"I'm sorry I put you through that, and I promise, from now on, I will always be there for you. And if I can't, I'll pray the angels watch over you."

Cecille smiles. "Angels? You really did get hurt in the head."

I smile too. "Maybe I'm finally getting things right in my

head."

Cecille wipes away the tears. "I don't know anything about angels, but I'll say this: Thank God, you're a terrible shot."

"Amen to that, sister." I grin. "Amen to that."

About the Author

A.J. Cattapan is a writer, teacher, and theater lover living in the Chicago area. Her love of the theater began in the sixth grade when her mother took her to see a production of *Guys and Dolls* at the local high school. That same year, her sixth grade reading teacher introduced her to *Anne of Green Gables*, and the dream to become a writer began. All things come full circle, and now she's a sixth grade reading and language arts teacher who hopes to inspire the next generation of writers.

You can follow her writing adventures at www.ajcattapan.com.

Acknowledgments

Thanks to Mom and Dad, who have never laughed at the crazy passions I've pursued. You two are my rocks, and I love you dearly.

Thanks to the best four brothers a girl could ever ask for, their wonderful wives who make great sisters-in-law, and the most adorable gang of nieces and nephews. God has truly blessed me with an amazing family.

Thanks to all of my writing pals over at ACFW, especially my local Chicago Area Chapter whose monthly meetings are a boost to my writing adrenaline.

An extra special thank you to the wonderful ACFW members who critiqued this manuscript through Scribes, particularly Gretchen E.K. Engel, Nanci Rubin, Beth Steury, and Pegg Thomas. I owe a great debt to those of you willing to take a peek at this manuscript. I was so fearful you'd find it too dark, but you embraced Nanette's story with open arms and gave me the courage to seek publication.

Dear Reader,

If you enjoyed reading Angelhood, I would appreciate it if you would help others enjoy this book, too. Here are some of the ways you can help spread the word:

Lend it. This book is lending enabled so please share it with a friend.

Recommend it. Help other readers find this book by recommending it to friends, readers' groups, book clubs, and discussion forums.

Share it. Let other readers know you've read the book by positing a note to your social media account and/or your Goodreads account.

Review it. Please tell others why you liked this book by reviewing it on your favorite ebook site like Amazon or Barnes and Noble and/or Goodreads.

Everything you do to help others learn about my book is greatly appreciated!

AJ Cattapan

Plan Your Next Escape!
What's Your Reading Pleasure?

Whether it's captivating historical romance, intriguing mysteries, young adult romance, illustrated children's books, or uplifting love stories, Vinspire Publishing has the adventure for you!

For a complete listing of books available, visit our website at www.vinspirepublishing.com.

Like us on Facebook at
www.facebook.com/VinspirePublishing
Follow us on Twitter at
www.twitter.com/vinspire2004
and join our newsletter for details of our upcoming releases, giveaways, and more! http://t.co/46UoTbVaWr

We are your travel guide to your next adventure!

Made in the USA
San Bernardino, CA
23 May 2016